HIS GIFT: PART ONE

PART ONE

A DARK BILLIONAIRE ROMANCE

By
Aubrey Dark

Chapter One

I breathe in the darkness.

There is a blindfold around my eyes. There is a collar around my neck. I am sitting up on my knees, naked, trembling. My wrists are bound to the bedposts, stretched out to either side of me.

He is behind me.

I can feel his breathing on the back of my neck. I strain forward, away from him. He is not touching me, but his breath is warm on my skin. I pull harder, but the ties around my wrists hold fast.

The ties around my wrist are silken handcuffs. The bed underneath me is covered in silk sheets. Even the blindfold is black silk.

Black. Everything is black. My eyes are open under the blindfold but I can see nothing. I sit there silently, feeling the air move against my naked body.

"Lacey, my darling." He breathes the words into my ear from behind me. I gasp as his hand touches my shoulder.

His fingers are long and slim. They are warmer than his breath on the back of my neck.

"Are you afraid of the dark?"

I shake my head. I won't give him the satisfaction of an answer.

Am I afraid of the dark? No, I want to say. I've always loved the dark. Even when I was a child, I didn't need a nightlight. I didn't shed a single tear when I broke my arm. I stayed in the haunted barn one night when my brothers dared me, and I didn't even cry out when my dad spanked me for doing it. My mom always said that I was the bravest girl she'd ever met.

Now, though, I don't feel brave. Now, in the darkness, I'm scared of what's going to happen. What he's going to do to me.

His fingers slide down my back. His other hand grips my hip and I feel the bed move as he shifts his weight closer to me. I grit my teeth.

Despite myself, I feel my body begin to respond as his hands curve down around my waist and pause there. Warmth spreads between my thighs. I clench them together tightly, trying to ignore the pulsing desire inside of me.

Take me. Take me.

No. This isn't me. This can't be real.

I jerk my head away at the sudden touch on my neck. Even in the darkness, I can tell that he is smiling behind me. The touch comes again, and this time I'm prepared. His lips press against my neck. I try to sit still, but an involuntary gasp comes from my mouth when he sucks gently on my skin.

"Oh, Lacey," he murmurs.

His hands come forward, sliding over my stomach and up to my breasts. Again he kisses my neck. Again I gasp. This time it's his tongue, the hot pressure sending me into near spasms as he cups my breasts.

He shifts his weight again, and now I moan as he sucks my skin and everything sinks into pure sensation—

2

—his muscled chest against my back, his skin hot against mine—

—his fingers pinching my nipples so hard it sends flames racing through my nerves, his thumb rolling over the hard swollen nubs—

—his lips taking me, his mouth possessing me, his tongue licking my skin—

—his breath whispering softness into my ear—

"I can't stop myself."

"Don't try."

I hear my voice rasping in the air. *Don't.* I don't want him to stop. Not now. I want him to do everything to me. I don't want him to hold back anymore.

His hands come down, gripping my thighs. His fingers scrabble needily over my skin. Before I can say another word, he forces my thighs apart. My body recoils, clenching together, but he's already kneeling between my legs behind me. I can feel his hard cock against the small of my back. It's impossibly hot, burning hot against my cool skin. I moan as he slides his cock down between my thighs to where I'm already slick with moisture.

"Jesus. Oh Jesus. Lacey." His voice is a growl that sends shivers through my body. "You don't know what you do to me."

My fingers grasp at the silk ties, but they are already pulled taut. My body, too, feels like it's pulled taut, waiting for his touch to send me into uncontrollable vibrations.

For a moment, before he enters me for the first time, I close my eyes. It doesn't matter; the blindfold is still on, but this feels like the last decision I make. I make it silently, the words curling through my mind and stopping before they reach my tongue.

Take me. Take me into your darkness.

Chapter Two

"Lacey, *please.*"

"Say pretty please."

"Pretty please with cream cheese frosting and a cherry on top."

My friend Steph looked at me across the cake table with eyes so round and pleading I finally understood why her boyfriend couldn't ever say no to her. Her red-gold eyelashes fluttered wildly and she gave me a cajoling grin. I sighed and licked the frosting off of the side of my cupcake.

"I wish I could, Steph," I said. "But I can't. I start my second job tonight."

"That shitty dive bar job over in East Manhattan?"

"That shitty dive bar job is going to pay my rent for this month," I pointed out. "And I just got off my waitress shift. I wanted to come over here and relax—"

"You came over here for the cupcakes."

"Cupcakes are part of relaxing!"

"It won't take long. The apartment building is like, ten blocks away. It'll take like ten minutes to deliver the cake if you walk."

"Short blocks or long blocks?" I couldn't believe she was getting me to do this for her.

"Short."

"Why can't you deliver it yourself?" I asked.

Stephanie pouted and I swear her blond ponytail pouted along with her, drooping down to one side.

"I have to be here to take the pans out when the timer goes off. I have three cakes going right now that have to be cooled and iced by tomorrow morning. You think you're the only one who works late nights?"

"Get Andy to do it."

"They said they wanted a girl to deliver it. Besides, I don't know where he is right now."

I gave her a look that said *Are You Serious?* She gave me a look that said *Yes, For Reals.*

"Steph, I'm exhausted—"

"I'll pay you."

At that, my ears perked up. My rent had just gone up in November, and my income hadn't. I'd finally managed to score a gig working as a bartender, but my first paycheck from that wouldn't come in until after my rent was due. A fact Stephanie was well aware of.

She waggled her eyebrows at me.

"Fine. Okay. How much?" I asked, slumping my chin down on my hand and taking another bite of the cupcake.

"Oh stop. You're not allowed to look sad when you're eating a cupcake."

"How much?"

"A hundred dollars."

I nearly choked on the cupcake.

"Seriously? For delivering a cake?" I said, coughing so hard I had to wipe tears from my eyes.

"Look, the guy paid two thousand for the cake. I don't want to fuck up the delivery."

"*What?*" My brain couldn't process the sentence for a moment. A hundred dollars would do a lot. Heck, that would get me through buying Christmas presents for my family. "Are there diamonds baked into the cake layers or what?"

"No. Well, kind of. The materials were super expensive. And it took me freaking forever to ice." Steph smiled a mischievous smile. "Wanna see it?"

There was a glint in her eyes that she always got when showing off a cake she was particularly proud of. When she brought the cake out of the fridge, though, I finally understood why she was so giddy about this one.

The cake itself wasn't that big—it was a round, two-tiered pan cake. I'd seen her make stuff that was way bigger and more impressive, structurally at least. But the icing...

"Criminy popsicles," I whispered.

Steph giggled at my Iowa version of swearing. I was agape. The cake glittered like it was made out of diamonds and gold. The icing itself was a pearly, shimmering white. Alongside the cake, curling up around both tiers, was what looked like a gold-stemmed branch of white orchids. Smaller flowers, these ones made out of gold, edged the circular rim of the cake plate.

I leaned forward to see the intricate gilding, but Steph stopped me with a hand on my shoulder.

"Careful," she said. "The icing will melt if you breathe too hard on it."

"That's icing?"

"All of it is icing. The orchids are a special fondant, but the little flowers are all gold leaf on top of icing. It took me all day to finish it."

"I bet," I said, sitting back in my seat. "Wow."

"Right? It's probably the coolest cake I'll ever make."

"Is it for a wedding?"

"No, weirdly enough, this one's for a birthday party. At least, that's what the guy said. Maybe it's for his wife."

"What building did you say it was going to?"

Steph grinned. She knew she had me.

"It's the penthouse suite in one of those bigshot highrises in the financial district. I bet you'll even get a tip for delivering it."

"Okay," I said, popping the last of the cupcake into my mouth and standing up from the cake table. "I'll do it."

"Awesome!" Steph clapped her hands. "Oh, and they said you have to wear a dress to deliver it."

"A dress?" I stopped in my tracks. "But—"

"I know, I know," she said. "You can borrow one of mine."

"Steph—"

"It's just for ten minutes. Please. I need your help with this, Lacey, or I wouldn't ask."

"How about *you* go and *I* take out the pans?"

Steph put her hands on her hips and glared at me. The last time I'd been in charge of taking the cakes out of the oven, they'd come out black. To be fair, I had forgotten to turn the volume down on my headphones. A cake timer going off sounded a lot like it belonged in the backing track of the latest Katy Perry album, really it did.

"Okay, I'll never offer to help you again in the bakery," I said, shaking my head.

"It's only a dress. It won't suddenly turn you into a girly girl, Lacey."

I looked at Steph, and then the cake. Thoughts of hundred dollar bills danced in my mind. Well, it *was* just for ten minutes.

"Fine," I grumbled. I hadn't worn a dress since my mom made me wear one to church the last time I visited her for Christmas. But this was for a good cause.

"Thank you so much! Oh Lacey, I don't know what I would do without you!"

"I bet Andy would be okay with wearing a dress," I said, arching one eyebrow.

"He'd probably be more comfortable in a dress than you would," Steph agreed. She put a glass cover over the two-tier cake. It settled around the cake like a globe protecting its contents. "But not half as sexy as you'll be!"

"Sexy?"

"Sexy. That's the only kind of dress I have. That's the only kind of dress you're allowed to wear in a New York City penthouse, I'm pretty sure. Heels, too."

"Oof. Let's get this over with," I said, casting one last glance at the cake sitting on the table. It glittered brightly under the fluorescent lights of the bakery.

"Get this over with? You get to go be sexy and deliver my cake to a party full of rich guys, and I have to sit here slaving in the kitchen. You should feel *lucky*."

"I'll feel luckier once I get back without tripping over my high heels and breaking my ankle."

"As long as you don't break it on the way there. That's my two thousand dollar masterpiece," Steph said.

***

Two thousand dollars.

"I can't believe I'm delivering a cake with a higher net worth than me," I said, tugging on the dress.

That was the other thing. Steph was curvy, but not like *I* was curvy. I had hips that stretched the fabric of her little black dress tight across my chest. My equally more-than-curvy chest.

"I can't wear this," I said.

"Why not?"

"It's a little black dress on you. It's an itty-bitty-teeny-weeny black dress on me. It's way too revealing."

"You can't be too revealing," Steph said. "That's like having too much cream cheese frosting. Impossible."

"Look at the front of this dress! It's so low-cut I could use it as a nipple sling if I wanted to."

"You look sexy."

"I look like one of those hippos from Fantasia." I flushed, pushing my boobs down into my bra to keep them from popping out completely.

"Let me get a shawl."

Steph dug through the top of her closet. By Manhattan standards, Steph's room was about average tiny, but she'd managed to score one of the few studios with a walk-in closet that hadn't been redesignated as a bedroom. Living right above the bakery was noisy as hell, which I minded more than she did.

In Iowa, where my parents lived, it was quiet. Like, fart in one room, hear it across the house quiet. I hadn't managed to get used to the hum and buzz of New York City yet, and so I slept with earplugs in, and headphones over the earplugs, in a cardboard box of an apartment in north Brooklyn as far away from the subway as I could.

"Here we are!" Steph waved a colorful shiny thing in the air.

"What's that?"

She shoved the rainbow-colored shawl over my head. It was knitted loosely. It was glittery and iridescent.

"It's an accessory."

"I'm not really into accessories. Although the Lisa Frank color scheme is attractive—"

"And it helps cover your boobs."

I looked up into the mirror. The rainbow iridescent shawl covered the tops of my shoulders. Its folds curved slowly across my chest, obscuring my cleavage.

"So it does. You have a point, my cupcake-wielding friend."

"Great. When you get back, I'll have a cupcake and your paycheck waiting for you."

"You're the best." I turned to go. Steph crossed her arms, blocking the doorway.

"What?" I asked.

She circled her finger in the air, telling me to turn around.

"Makeup."

"I have makeup on," I protested.

"You have concealer on, and only because I convinced you that you needed to hide the circles under your eyes for an interview."

"That's totally makeup."

"Sit."

I sat.

"I swear, Lacey," she said, "If you put half the amount of effort into painting your face as you put into painting graffiti—"

"It's called street art," I interrupted her.

"Street art. Right. Like that one big vagina flower you painted on one of the A-line cars."

"That was inspired by Georgia O'Keefe!" I cried.

"Did you have to paint it on a subway car?"

"If you want to buy me a ten by thirty foot canvas, by all means," I said.

"Ten by thirty?" Steph whistled. "That's bigger than my apartment."

"See? How am I supposed to do art here? I can't afford it! Now, when I have a gallery to put my art in—"

"Sure, okay, okay," Steph said, poising a brush just over my nose. I looked at it cross-eyed. "Hold still. This won't hurt a bit."

"I don't believe you. You'll torture me."

"It's not torture, it's art. You do your art on subway cars, I'll do mine on cakes and faces," Steph said. "Okay?"

I would have nodded, but she was already dabbing something onto my face with a cotton pad and I was afraid to move.

There were so many powders and brushes flying across my face that I lost track of whether I was supposed to be closing my eyes or pressing my lips together. She lined my eyes and then she lined my lips. When I asked if she wanted to line anything else, she pursed her lips in disapproval. By the time the cake timer went off downstairs, we were both running out of patience with each other.

"I guess that'll have to do," Steph said, eyeing me critically.

"That's the sweetest thing anyone's ever said to me."

"Oh, go deliver a cake, why don't you?"

I smirked and made a mock curtsey.

"My pleasure."

She blew me a kiss, and I blew one right back. I was feeling like a hundred bucks.

Sure, I was in a dress so tight it made my butt look like J-Lo's. Sure, I was inch-deep in skin foundation and mascara. And sure, I'd have to get out of all of it before going to my second job.

But this was going to be the easiest hundred bucks I'd ever make.

Chapter Three

Tottering down Seventh Avenue with a two-thousand dollar cake perched precariously in my hands, I grimaced at yet another catcall. The chilly air didn't bother me half as much as the idiot men who couldn't stop yelling at me.

This was why I never wore dresses.

"Hey baby, looking tight!"

"Wanna come back to my place?"

I scowled, looking away from the guys who were calling after me. Most of the time, I wore a sweatshirt and baggy jeans to go out. Steph called it my "hoodlum chic" but I called it peace and quiet. Also, you can't hide paint markers in skinny jeans.

Up ahead, two teenage boys whistled at me.

"Yo fatso, who'd you eat?"

"Your mom. She loved it," I said, raising my eyebrows as I strutted past the one who'd called out. His friend burst out laughing and punched him in the shoulder. He sputtered angrily.

If it had been any other day, I would have welcomed a brawl with a scrawny teenager. I knew self-defense as well as any girl, and my punches had some power behind them. But tonight was different.

Tonight I was delivering a cake. The fanciest cake in the world.

Not wanting to risk squishing the cake, I spent most of the walk on the curb, dodging the groups of pedestrians that threatened to surround me. Finally I turned onto the street Steph had sent me to.

Craning my neck, I looked down at the directions. Then back up. Then back down.

This was a *scene*. In front of the building, a line of cars waited to be valet parked. Each one was more expensive than the other. I saw a Ferrari, two Maseratis, one of the new super Teslas, and a car I thought I recognized from the latest Batman movie. It was incredible.

I stopped for a moment, gathering my senses and trying to figure out the easiest way to get into the building without being crushed by the mob of people gawking outside the door. Elevators whooshed up and down the outside of the upscale highrise.

A woman jostled my elbow and I instinctively pulled back, cradling Steph's cake.

"Hey, watch it!" I said.

"Excuse me?" A six-foot tall blonde stick figure stared down at me contemptuously. Her eyes swept over my figure. "It looks like *you* should be the one watching out."

I swallowed, my mouth suddenly dry.

Obnoxious guys I could handle. They were just like a more annoying version of my brothers. Tease me, and I'd tease them right back. It was the same with my art buddies who tagged alongside me, occasionally helping me throw up some of my bigger pieces. They poked at me without pushing any of my buttons.

But bullies? Especially female bullies? I couldn't take them. Maybe it was being bullied through my preteens. It had gotten so bad that I was taking more sick days off of school than going. My parents eventually pulled me out of school and I finished my GED on my own.

Whenever another woman looked at me with *that look,* something inside of me turned back into a little girl, and not the brave one my mom knew. The scared one who ran and hid in the bathroom to cry during class.

Another benefit to not wearing makeup: you don't utterly mess up your face with mascara when you cry.

"I thought all the whores stayed in the bad part of the city," she murmured to her friend, just loud enough that I could hear.

My face turned bright red and I turned away quickly, hugging the cake in my arms. My Iowa upbringing had done nothing to prepare me for being called a whore by another woman.

"Are you girls going up to the party?"

A man dressed in an expensive looking suit waved in my direction. I stepped forward, making sure to avoid the blonde supermodel who'd called me a whore.

"Please come through this way," he said, motioning to a side entrance. I hung back and went through the doorway near to last. All of the other girls were dressed in gorgeous gowns of every color, and they were all at least half a foot taller than me, in even taller heels. It was a parade of models.

I slunk in after them, holding the cake in front of me like a shield. There was a good reason I was there. Even if I wasn't a runway model. I held my head high.

This was a two thousand dollar cake I was carrying, after all.

The girls congregated near a table at the end of the hallway. The table was covered in clipboards.

"Everyone must sign the waiver form before going up to the elevator," the man said. He sounded bored.

I set the cake down carefully on the edge of the table that was empty, and picked up one of the clipboards.

The form was three pages long, and all of the other girls were busy initialing and signing in the appropriate spots. I glanced down at the first page.

"...signee agrees to waive all personal liability on account of the owner..."

"...in signing, agrees to complete non-disclosure under severe penalty and prosecution of law..."

"...strict dress code, enforceable and negotiable only at the discretion of the owner..."

I flipped to the next page. Things got even weirder.

"...will not speak unless spoken to..."

"...signee must obey all orders given..."

I looked up to see the first few girls already handing their forms in. They gathered near a marble elevator door where the man in the suit motioned them toward. The elevator doors opened and the girls disappeared into the building.

I picked up Steph's cake and stepped forward to the man in the suit.

"Excuse me," I said. "Is this the entrance for the party—"

"Is your form done?"

"Uh, no. Do I need to do that? I'm just—"

"Everyone needs to fill out the form," the man said. He looked down at me with irritation. "Or you can find another way up."

"Sure," I said, slinking back to the table. Whatever. I just needed to get in and out so I could get to my new job.

Everybody else was finishing up and there were only a few clipboards left. I grabbed one and signed all of the blank spots quickly, then handed it over to the man in the suit.

"On the elevator, please," he said. I got in, pressing myself back against the side of the elevator along with a half dozen other girls. The elevator swooped upwards quickly, leaving my stomach down on the first floor.

The elevator was made of glass, and as we lifted past the first few stories I gasped. I hadn't realized what was so obvious. If I could see the elevators from outside, the elevators could see out.

I could see all of New York!

The elevator shaft was made of glass panels, and we looked out onto the city with all its glimmering lights and narrow alleys where darkness hides. The floor, too, was glass.

Oh, jeez.

My palms turned clammy with fear. All of the blood in my body sucked down into my feet, and I felt like I was going to collapse. God, I felt so vulnerable in a dress.

I couldn't run in heels. As we rose higher and higher, I gulped air and tried not to look directly down.

My fingers were sweating, but I held the cake firmly in my grasp. I was not going to let anything get in the way of delivering this cake successfully. Steph was counting on me.

I heard a giggle, and looked up to see the tall blonde woman staring daggers at me. Her friend was the one laughing. I flushed again and averted my eyes.

"You're not going to the party, are you?" the friend said. She wasn't—yep. She was talking to me.

"I'm just delivering this to the kitchen," I said, in as confident a tone as I could muster. I felt like throwing up. The only thing holding me back was the thought of ruining a two thousand dollar cake with puke.

"Right. The kitchen." The girl rolled her eyes, and Blondie dissolved into giggles. I turned my head to look away from them.

Bad idea. From so high up, the people down on the street looked like ants. The cars looked like tiny Hot Wheels versions of themselves. And I was way, *way* too high up.

"Scared of heights?"

I looked up to see another one of the supermodels whispering at me. She didn't look like she was making fun of me, though. Heck, she looked just as green around the gills as I did.

"Yeah," I said. "A little. You?"

"I'm terrified of heights," she said. I noticed then that her hands were clutching the rail. Her fingers were white with pressure.

"It's alright," I said. "They probably spent a million dollars on this elevator. No way would it ever break and send us all flying down to our deaths. It would be a publicity nightmare. Right?"

Her mouth dropped open. She stared at me in terror. Okay, so maybe that wasn't the most comforting thing ever to say. Fortunately, the elevator stopped just then and the doors opened. I felt my heart rise back up into my chest as I tottered shakily out of the elevator.

"Alright," I said to myself, trying to get my head back into the game. "Deliver the cake. Deliver the—"

As I walked out into the top-floor penthouse, I forgot all about what I was here to do. My legs stopped working and I just stood there gaping. There really were no words for it, but one of my mom's old phrases came into my head and so that's what came out of my mouth.

"Jesus's jumping jelly beans!"

***

I stared out across a huge room. Every square inch of the place glittered and shone. Crystal chandeliers lined the ceiling, sending their glowing light out onto the floor that hummed with hundreds of people, all dressed in evening gowns and tuxedos. Something about it seemed strange to me, but I was too much in awe to figure it out. The art on the walls. The servers gliding through the masses of chatting partygoers.

And the ice sculptures!

Near me, a towering ice sculpture arched over the hallway. It was an angel wrestling with a demon, and their hands were locked together as they stared into each other's eyes. It was gorgeous, a sculptural masterpiece. It should have been in the museum of contemporary art, but instead here it was, melting in some rich guy's apartment. Nobody was even looking at it!

Another man in a tuxedo was talking to the supermodels, and when he saw me he motioned me over angrily.

"Sign in here before you go inside," he said, pointing to another clipboard. "Leave your ID in this case with me. And put on a collar."

He held out a red leather collar in my direction. I just stared at him. Apart from having both of my hands occupied with holding a cake, I was totally weirded out by his request.

A collar?

That was when I realized what was weird about the party going on. All of the women were wearing collars. I gazed around. Some of the women had thin black bands around their necks. Others had chunky gold collars ornamented with diamond studs. And the supermodels were all fitting collars around their necks, too.

"What the *heck?*" I murmured. Was this some sort of bondage orgy thing for millionaires? I had no idea what was going on.

The man looked like he wanted to send me back down the elevator, or perhaps throw me off of a balcony to get me away from him sooner. Fortunately, the supermodels spoke up.

"She's not with us," the bitchy blond girl interrupted.

"Yeah," her friend echoed. "She's going to the *kitchen*."

The man frowned at me.

"Cake delivery," I explained, holding up Steph's creation.

"Yes, yes," the man said, clearly irritated at having to deal with me. "Down the hall and to your left. But leave through the servants' exit, please."

I didn't bother asking him where the servants' exit was. It would be easier to just ask someone once I got to where I was supposed to be going. I turned around and exhaled, thankful that I didn't have to deal with collars or supermodels anymore.

Me? I was just delivering a cake.

Chapter Four

I wandered off underneath the ice sculpture of the angel and demon. The ice was melting, and water dripped off of the ends of the angel's wings. Passing through, I continued walking along the outskirts of the party, the cake box clasped in my hand.

The hallway led out of the main room. As I walked away, the noise of the party grew quiet. Here, the hall was paneled with thick oak. Crushed velvet drapes framed sculptures—these ones made out of a more permanent marble—and the ceiling was vaulted with gilded wood ornamentation. Whoever this rich guy was, he had a taste for antique design.

As I was walking past the first door on the left, I heard a noise. That wasn't the kitchen, was it? I pulled the door open with one hand, holding the cake with the other. I poked in my head.

"Oh!" I cried. The room I'd opened up was a den of some kind, with leather sofas and books lining the walls. There was a pool table in the middle of the room.

And on the pool table, a woman lay on her back. The man standing at the far end of the table looked up at me, his pants around his ankles. His tie fluttered over her ample cleavage as he bent over her, between her legs.

From his expression, he was busy putting *something* into a pocket. When he saw me, his eyes widened only slightly in irritated surprise.

"Room's occupied," the man grunted.

"Unless you want to join," the woman said, looking at me from upside down.

"Uh… no. No thank you. Sorry to interrupt," I said, a fierce shame burning on my cheeks. I closed the door quickly behind me.

I made my way down to the end of the hall. From the left, waiters streamed out of a door. Okay. That was the kitchen. I was almost there when something caught my eye.

No way.

I snuck over to the door across the hall from the kitchen. It was ajar, and inside I had caught a glimpse of something.

But no, it couldn't be.

One of my favorite graffiti artists in NYC had stopped putting anything up in the city two years ago. Nobody knew who he was apart from his tag—he signed all of his pieces with the name "Kage." I'd tried to catch him in the act of tagging, lots of people had, but he was invisible.

His letters flowed like water, like sunlight through tree branches. When he painted a wall, nobody ever dared paint over it. That was how good he was. His pieces grew out of cracks in the brick, like his paint was a force of nature finding a way to flow out and into the world. Every painting he did was perfectly suited to the place he put it. It was as though the ugly bare walls had been waiting for him to come along and make them beautiful again.

I'd pored over his work, finding his stuff posted online and going to visit some of his pieces in person. He liked to throw his bigger pieces up in the alleyways downtown rather than in the subway. Much more dangerous. Much more risky. Maybe he had finally gotten caught, and that's why he wasn't painting anymore.

Now, though, staring me in the face was a painting by him that I had never seen before. I darted a glance back over at the kitchen door, swinging shut after another tuxedoed waiter passed through.

I had time, didn't I?

I always had time for art. Just a peek, and I'd be back to deliver the cake. Then back to Steph's to change, another ten minutes to get to my job… yeah, sure. I had plenty of time.

Pushing the door open, I stepped inside of the dimly lit room. There was nobody in the front of this room, although it looked like the room continued on through another doorway. The painting by Kage took up most of the wall, lit up by a single spotlight from below. I took a step closer and—

"Ohh!"

My heel sunk into the carpet and caught there, sending me tumbling forward. I lunged forward and caught the cake before it fell, but I heard the contents shift inside the box.

"Stupid heels! Stupid, stupid," I repeated. I kicked both of my heels off quickly and set the cake down on the carpet. I opened it up, praying it hadn't gotten messed up.

"Oh no. Oh no."

I bit my lip and looked closer. One of the orchid branches had bent, it looked like. The flower petals were digging into the gold icing on top. I reached in and pried back the fake flower, only to have the gold lift away on my fingertip. Frowning, I pushed the flower back. It didn't look wrong like that. Maybe a little *different* from the one Steph had finished, but not *bad*.

I closed the lid, picked the cake back up, and was debating whether to enter the kitchen barefoot when I heard a noise.

"Hello?" I whispered. The rooms in here seemed so dim that I couldn't imagine anyone from the party would be inside. But I had heard *something*.

I stepped inside, edging my way across the room. I still held the cake box in my hands, but it was easier to creep barefoot on the plush carpet. My toes sank down into the lush fibers.

"Hello?" I said, a bit louder. Then I poked my head around the doorway into the next room.

"Wow."

This wasn't a bedroom or a kitchen. This wasn't just another ordinary part of the house.

It was an art gallery.

I gaped at the paintings that filled the walls of the room. There were a dozen or so large canvases hanging from steel wires in the middle of the room. The canvases were big, and hung a couple of feet above the floor, creating a sort of viewing maze. And there, in the middle—

Another painting… by him.

I walked forward, holding the cake still, but my attention was entirely on the canvas in front of me.

KAGE. This was all lettering, none of the decoration that marked his other pieces. But there was no need for decoration, no need for any ornaments or frills. The lettering was art already. The broad swoop of the first letter carried over through the name, and each letter seemed to flow through to the next with a hundred small tendrils, all green and gold and vibrant. It felt natural. It felt real.

This was what I was shooting for every time I put up a flower. I wanted this—to be able to make the art seem as though it was growing out of the canvas on its own. The art was composed of the letters of the artist's name, but the artist was invisible in the art itself.

When my mom scolded me for painting graffiti on our fences, I couldn't explain why I was doing what I was doing. But this painting, this piece of art, made sense to me in a way that nothing else could. I couldn't do watercolor postcard-sized paintings and hope to have this effect.

Kage's art was big; it *loomed*. It was meant to fill this space.

Looking up at the painting, I was too distracted to notice anything until I saw his shoes.

It was a man, standing on the other side of the painting. If the canvas hadn't been there, he could have reached out and touched me. I didn't know where he had come from.

In my shock, I gasped... and my hands slipped. The cake box that I had carried for blocks and blocks in high heels, the cake box I'd clenched all the way up the insanely scary elevator—it slid out of my grasp.

I could only watch in horror as the cake box opened and Steph's two-thousand dollar masterpiece split in half, the top layer of cake falling upside down onto the plush carpet.

Oh dear Lord. Oh my sweet jelly bean Jesus.

What had I done? I stood stock still, my fingers splayed outward as though I might be able to reverse time and put the cake back together. I didn't want to be here. This wasn't happening. Two thousand dollars. This was a nightmare.

Then I heard his voice come from behind the canvas. It was a voice so booming and low that it made goosebumps run along my arms.

"Who are you?"

***

I couldn't see any of him but his shoes and an ankle's worth of pant leg. His shoes were black, polished. Shiny. A fleck of gold icing had flown off of the cake I'd just dropped and landed on his left shoe. I swallowed.

Oh Lord. Steph is going to kill me. And if she doesn't kill me, this rich guy will definitely kill me when he sees I got cake frosting on him.

"Who are you?" he asked again. He made no movement to walk around the canvas to see me.

"Who are *you*?" I asked, staring straight ahead at the canvas. The best defense was a good offense, after all, and I had no idea what else to say.

"Did you come here for the birthday party?" he asked.

"Um. Yes?"

"That's for me. It's my birthday."

I was over being shocked. Now I was well into shame. I could feel the heat rising off of my cheeks. I blew out a breath.

"Oh. Uh, Happy Birthday," I said. "I'm sorry. About all this. I—"

"Why are you standing there?"

"Here?" I looked around. I was in the middle of the canvases. In front of me, I could see the detailing on the word KAGE. The curling end of the letter K split off into a forest of branches that tangled into the letter A.

"In my art gallery," the man said. His voice was a growl. "In front of this piece."

"I wanted to see the Kage painting," I said. My mouth was dry and shame burned my skin. At least he wasn't yelling at me about the birthday cake. Yet.

"The Kage painting? Why?"

"I... I haven't seen his stuff in a while. He quit tagging a couple years ago, didn't he?"

There was a pause. I looked down at the man's shoes again. He hadn't moved at all, and I wondered what he looked like behind the canvas. A silver-haired businessman, probably. But his voice was so deep—

"Are you an art student?"

"Me?" I snorted nervously. "Yeah, no, I wish I had the money to sit around all day doing that."

"So you're a painter?"

I opened my mouth and couldn't find anything to say. If you asked my parents, my best friend, my brothers, they would all say that I was a painter. I loved to paint. I'd been tagging from the time I was two and got into my mom's lipstick.

But there was a seriousness in his voice that made me hesitate to call myself a painter. Was I, really? Some people would call me nothing more than a vandal. Even if I put my paint on canvases, it wouldn't measure up.

Looking in front of me, staring at the amazing Kage painting, I couldn't say it.

"I... try," I said.

"You try to paint, but no colors come out?"

"Ha. Ha. I try to paint *well*. I'm not a painter like this guy, though," I said, gesturing forward as though he could see.

Jeez. It was weird to be having a conversation *through* the canvas of a painting. Let alone this painting.

"What do you mean by that?"

"I'm not talented like he is."

"You have no talent?"

"Well, not none. But this kind of work..." I trailed off.

"What do you like about it?" the man asked.

Although his voice was low, he didn't seem angry. Or upset. If someone spilled a two-thousand-dollar cake onto my probably-more-than-two-thousand-dollar carpet, I would definitely be upset. But there was no hint of it in his voice. It made me breathe a bit easier.

I looked at the canvas in front of me. All of the qualities that had drawn me to the piece seemed silly to say aloud. I licked my lips.

"Uh, it's... it's perfect." A burst of nervous laughter came from my lips. "I mean, really. Every line. It's all perfect, it all needs to be there. It feels like every part of it should be there. And the lines are all so precise, but they add up to something that looks so organic. I, uh…" I faltered, not getting any visual feedback at all. "I just really like it," I finished lamely.

"I see."

"Where'd you get it? Was it a commission, or—"

"*Who* are you?"

"Uh," I said, fear creeping back into my heart at the sound of his voice. "I'm Lacey."

"Come around the canvas now, Lacey. I want to see you."

The way he spoke the words, it wasn't an order. It was just the tone of a man who had never been disobeyed. I found myself moving before I meant to move. I reached the edge of the canvas and hesitated.

"Come."

Chapter Five

The man standing on the other side of the canvas looked up at me with something like surprise in his eyes.

He must have been shocked to see me after the parade of supermodels, I suppose. And I was shocked, too.

"You're *young*!" I exclaimed.

"Excuse me?" he said, his eyebrow arching.

"I mean, you're not old. I mean, I thought you were. Older. That is."

Not only was he not old, he was *hot*. His eyes shone like green emeralds from under his dark, perfectly coiffed hair. He was wearing a dark gray tailored suit that fit his lines, accentuating his height and his broad chest. When he looked down at me, I had the strangest feeling that he was taking a picture.

"Sorry again," I said.

"Lucas said that he was sending me something," the man said.

"Oh, the—ah, the cake—"

"But where's your collar?"

He tilted his head at me.

"Yeah, about that," I said. "I'm not really into accessories. And I was just here to—"

"Where do you think you are?"

My mouth opened and closed like a mentally challenged goldfish.

"I—well, this is the top floor of the building—nice place, by the way—"

"This is my birthday party," he said, answering his own question.

"Oh. Sure."

"What have you heard about me?" he asked.

"You? What's your name?"

The man smiled, the slow curve moving across his lips in a casual ripple of amusement.

"Jake Carville. Have you never heard of me before?"

"Uh, no. Sorry," I said again. I felt like I was apologizing for everything. I deserved it, after all. "About the cake—"

"I'll get someone to clean it up. Don't worry." The man waved his hand, as though he didn't realize that it was a two thousand dollar cake. Then again, maybe he didn't care. A flicker of hope bloomed in my chest.

"Then you really don't know who I am," he was saying.

"No." I shook my head, trying to remember if I'd ever heard of a Jake Carville. I didn't really follow the news, and I couldn't afford cable TV. He could have been anything—an NBC executive, a Wall Street guru, a congressman—but I had no idea.

"Lucas did go out of his way, didn't he?" he murmured. He stepped closer to me, and all of the breath ran out of my body. His cologne smelled faintly of peppermint, and as he leaned down to me I tried my best to stand tall. Even though I was barefoot.

"Lucas?" Steph hadn't mentioned a Lucas.

"You're very innocent," he said. He lifted his hand and traced the line of my chin with one finger. His touch shocked me with its possessiveness. If it had been any other man, I'd have clocked him in the face at the first touch. But he was so... so calm.

"Not as innocent as you'd think," I said, lifting my chin defiantly.

"No?" His thumb pressed my lower lip, making my lips part.

I felt a rush of heat down between my thighs. His fingers were strong, but his caress was gentle. I wanted to lean my head into his touch. I wanted to kiss his thumb and suck the salt off of his skin.

His eyes burned a deep, rich green and I could smell his aftershave as he came closer. I trembled as he put his hand on my shoulder and held me still as he stepped behind me.

What was happening right now? I didn't understand what the heck this guy was doing, or what he wanted. One hand kneaded my shoulder gently as he moved out of my sight. His other hand came around my waist and rested on my hip.

His fingers trailed down from my shoulder, his fingertips grazing the back of my arm. I shivered. I wasn't about to move, but my entire body was ready to jump as I felt his hands press on either side of my hips.

"This dress doesn't fit you," he said.

I gulped a breath.

"I—I know. It's my friend's dress," I said.

He stepped closer to me. He didn't touch me with anything but his hands, but I could tell that he was closer.

His body heat radiated through the air between us, and his breath was warm on my neck.

"Take it off."

***

"Excuse me?" I couldn't believe that I had heard him correctly.

"Take it off."

"Excuse me?"

"You're excused for your insolence," Jake growled. "Now take off the damn dress."

Before I could figure out how to respond, he pulled me backwards. I fell off balance and landed against his chest. His arms wrapped around me. His muscles were hard and—

Oh, Lord, his cock was hard, too. He was pressed up against me from behind and I could feel it, thick and throbbing against my lower back. My heart pounded in my ears and all the room seemed to spin.

This wasn't... I couldn't. I really couldn't.

I was a virgin.

He couldn't have known it, of course. I had no idea what to do with a guy. I mean, I had an idea, but nothing specific or detailed. I'd never even gone past second base with anyone.

And now he was acting like he wanted... well, I couldn't imagine what he wanted. More than I was capable of, that's for sure.

"Lacey."

I took off the shawl. Already I felt bare. My cleavage was full to bursting out of the front.

"Now the dress," he said.

I reached up as though in a dream and tugged on the zipper. I didn't know how to stop him. Even the idea of asking him to stop seemed completely absurd, as though it was impossible not to follow his orders. That was how absolutely in control he was.

Steph had told me once, one night when we were staying up late and drinking wine with our cupcakes, that I ought to find a mature man who, in her words, "knew what the hell to do with your body."

Well, heck, I'd thought. I didn't even know what to do with my body. How could a man have any idea what to do with me? Now, though, with Jake standing behind me, I knew exactly what Steph meant. Because this man knew what he wanted. He would know what the hell to do with my body.

Once he saw what was under the dress, he might not want me anymore, though. And hey, as long as I got out of here alive, that was fine by me. But as I peeled the dress down over my body, I found myself hoping that he wouldn't kick me out. Even with my blue bra and black panties mismatching.

I found myself hoping that he would want to keep me.

Could I do this? Could I lose my virginity to some random man? Even if he was handsome as sin and richer than the world?

The dress fell down to my bare feet. Swallowing the lump in my throat, I turned to face him. He looked down, taking my body in an inch at a time. It was so long before he looked up at me, his lips parting slowly. He looked *hungry*.

"Take off your bra."

"I... I don't..."

"You don't want to?"

He had me there. I wanted to. The desire in his eyes scared me, but it also made me feel something that I hadn't felt before.

Lord, I felt so *wanted*.

"Take it off."

I turned my back to him and unhooked my bra. Then I let it drop to the floor along with my dress. With my toes, I delicately kicked it away.

Then I crossed my arms over my chest and turned back around.

"You're a temptress," Jake growled.

There, again. That low thrum in his voice that turned my insides to thick cream.

"I didn't think a man like you could be tempted."

"By this? By you? Oh, Lacey. *Lacey*."

Before I could react, he was in front of me. Jake raced his hand down my arm, skimming my bare hip. It came to a rest cupping the outside curve of my ass. I bit down hard on my lip, trying to push back the feelings that tangled through my body and tore at my nerves.

What was I doing? Why was I obeying him?

Was it the soft animal whisper in his voice that said I want you? Was it that which tempted me?

"Jake."

It was the first time I'd said his name. It seemed to stun him. His fingers froze their caress.

"Why did you call me that?" he asked.

"Your… it's your name."

"Don't use my name."

"What?" I furrowed my brows, confused. "Then what do I call y—"

"Don't call me anything."

"Don't call you anything?" I repeated.

"You can call me Sir. But only if you must. Otherwise, try not to use my name."

"I'll try."

That, at least, was one thing I could do. I could try to do this for him, no matter how weird it seemed. *Don't call him Jake. Alright.*

"Let me see you, Lacey."

"Should I… I mean, are we in private? The door's not locked." I bit my lip, a nervous thrill of fear sending strong vibrations through my nervous system.

"Does that matter to you?"

"What? Wh—yes! Of course it matters."

"I'm a stranger to you," he said. "Isn't that right?"

"Yes."

"And another stranger seeing you, wouldn't that be the same?"

NO!

The voice in my head was louder than anything, even instinct. It sang through my skull.

No, it wouldn't be the same.

No, you're more than that.

You are different.

Different. Yes. There was a calm confidence to him that I still couldn't place a finger on. He stood, his

41

fingers stroking my skin in a slow contemplation. It seemed as though he was living entirely in this one moment, his senses soaking in all of the room. Soaking in *me*.

"If I'd known I was going to be putting on a show tonight, I would have worn matching underwear," I said, smiling weakly.

"You're doing fine," he said. "More than fine."

His eyes ate me up; they gnawed my body.

"I want to show you off," he said.

"What?" Show me off?

"I want to peel you naked and lay you down in front of a hundred people and take you for myself. I want to lick your hot cunt."

"Sir."

The word was a shadow of a gasp. I had no breath in me. No, it wasn't only one breath. It was the whole world. All of the air was gone and I was gasping at nothing.

The walls spun. I blinked, then again, trying to focus.

"Forgive me for being so blunt this early with you. I'm sure you'll understand."

"I have to go."

The words tore from my throat. Jake stared at me with a blank look on his face.

"See, I have a new job," I said, sputtering as I bent down to pick up the bra. I kept one arm covering my breasts. How effective it was, I didn't know. I wasn't about to look up before I had both arms crossed in front of me again. "I'm starting tonight, after I leave here."

"Who says you're leaving?"

His eyes turned dark.

"What do you mean? *I* say I'm leaving. That's how it works," I said. I pulled on my bra and had my dress up around my shoulders in two seconds.

"Lacey, you aren't leaving."

He said it kindly, but there was a certainty to the statement that made my pulse thud harder.

"You're starting to scare me," I warned. It wasn't fear, though, that ran through me.

"Good. I'll like that. I think you'll like it, too."

"What?"

"Don't worry. I'll take very good care of you. If I scare you, you'll enjoy it."

His tongue slipped over his bottom lip, wetting it. I couldn't help but imagine what he would taste like. Mint and spice, rough like cinnamon bark.

It felt insane. I stood there calmly, barefoot. This man, this stranger had just seen me as close to naked as anyone ever had. And now he was telling me that he wanted to scare me.

Instead of fear, I felt stabs of curiosity when he spoke. He didn't seem like he would hurt me. He seemed so calm, so assured. It was... it was *thrilling*.

I zipped up my dress quickly and tugged the hem back down around my hips.

"Really, though. I have to go."

"I'll let you go on one condition."

"A condition?" I tilted my chin up toward his face. His cool emerald irises shimmered with silver specks. His eyes were cold, but his gaze burned my skin.

43

"Only one condition."

"What is it?"

"Let me make you come."

He smiled slowly, letting his words sink into me.

"*Then*," he said, "I'll let you go."

Chapter Six

"Make… make me…"

"Make you come."

"I'm not getting naked again—"

"I'm not asking you to. I told you I would take good care of you. First, I want you to come back into the gallery with me."

"The gallery?" I nodded. "Okay."

His finger stroked once down my neck, and he turned to me with an irritated look.

"Oh," he said. "I'd forgotten you didn't have your collar."

"I don't wear a collar."

"You will," he said, waving his hand in the air as though it was a commonplace thing. "But now, I want to talk with you about this cake."

Oh, crud on a muffin. The cake.

I'd almost forgotten about it in the minutes since Jake had looked at my body and told me to strip for him. Everything seemed like a daydream, but seeing the cake on its side pulled me back to reality with a sharp yank.

Right. A two thousand dollar mistake.

"You need to pick this up," Jake said. His voice was even and low.

"Of course," I said. "I'm so sorry." A bright flush swept over the top part of my cheeks. My eyes watered with the heat.

"Don't be ashamed. Apologize and find pleasure in picking it up."

"Pleasure?" I stared down at the flattened cake. It had broken open in the top layer, and I saw that it was red velvet cake under the gold icing.

"First apologize."

"I'm sorry," I repeated.

"Then pick it up."

I bent down and gingerly picked up the sides of the cake box. Some of the icing had spattered onto the carpet, but the cake was mostly still contained. I supported the bottom with one hand and stood up.

"Is there a trash can somewhere?" I asked. "Or… I mean…"

"Put it on that side table."

I obeyed his instruction. All the while, his words whirled in my mind: *I will make you come.* His breath was a rasp that sent a tremor through me. I could hear my heartbeat behind his words. My pulse was racing.

"What are you thinking about?"

I looked up. On the wall above the side table, there was a mirror. I could see Jake's reflection in it. He was staring at the back of my head intently.

"Nothing," I said quickly.

"What was it?"

I blushed. I wasn't going to tell him. No way.

"Were you thinking about me?"

"You're arrogant, aren't you?"

He whipped me around so fast that I tripped over my own feet. I stumbled and he caught me, pinning me back against the mirror. My hip was pressed against the side table. I couldn't move.

"Me?"

He shot a glance down at the broken cake.

"This cake, who paid for it? Was it you?"

"N—no."

"Who paid for this party? All of it?"

"You did."

"I want to enjoy tonight. I want to enjoy everything that has been given to me, because I have paid for every last ounce of pleasure," he said, his voice throttled down. The words resonated down through his chest.

"I have paid dearly for this. And I will take what I want, when I want."

His arm reached around my back and pulled me up against his body. I cried out as he squeezed my hips. His fingers gripped my ass.

"You are a gift that I paid for," he said. "You are a treasure. I want to treasure you."

As he spoke, his hands pulled me even closer. They clasped my hips and caressed my shoulders. They tugged my thigh against him, and Lord, oh Lordy, he was hard. I melted inside as he rubbed slowly, sensuously, against the front of my body.

He was so tall that his lips brushed my hairline. *Oh God, I hope I remembered to shampoo last night.*

How crazy was I? If I had thought about it, I should have screamed my head off. I should have shoved him away. But desire burned through me so hot and bright that I ignored my rational side. Damn the consequences. I

had been pure for my whole life, and now I needed this...
this dark, sinful thing. I wanted his desire.

His lips brushed my skin only lightly at my
forehead. His fingers, though, brushed over my mouth and
pinched the line of my chin.

"Lacey, you sweet delicious thing."

He reached out to the broken cake. He swept one
finger through the gold icing and brought it up to my face.

"Suck it off."

My eyes flickered back and forth from his iced
finger to his stern face.

"Lacey, you're being needlessly slow about
following my orders."

"It's just... I'm just not sure about this. I mean—
"

"Not sure?"

His eyes narrowed. His eyebrows slanted dark,
twin bolts of black down his face.

"I don't know—"

He shoved me back hard against the wall. My
breath went out with one solid *whoosh*. I gasped.

"Don't know?"

Jake put his finger to my lips, smearing icing onto
my mouth.

"Take it. Suck it."

I opened my mouth and he thrust his fingers
inside, hard. My hands clutched at his wrists. My mouth
was full, the icing dripping down my throat.

At the same time, his other hand came down and
slid under my dress. I screamed from behind his hand, but

his fingers turned my scream into a moan. I clenched my thighs together, but his hand was too strong.

"Suck it. Lick it," he whispered. His mouth was against my ear, and his whole body pinned mine against the wall. I couldn't reach him with my arms held back, and his one hand was working its way between my thighs.

Tears watered my eyes. I moaned as he hooked one finger up around my panties, brushing me down there.

"You're hot already, aren't you, Lacey? Good girl. Already so nice and wet."

"*Mmm!*" I cried out, shaking my head. "*Mmm!*"

"God, you're the best gift. Almost perfect. A bit too hesitant at times. But I'll train that out of you."

"Mmm—oh!"

My cry came as he slid his hand deeper. He curled his fingers, and God, oh God, he was inside me. His palm pressed against my clit, hot and wet.

I froze.

Nothing had prepared me for this. I'd read books, I'd watched porn. And I'd touched myself a few times, after my friends convinced me that my parents were being way old fashioned by calling it a sin. But nothing I had done or seen had prepared me for the quiet flicker of pleasure that danced through my body just then.

"Ah!"

I cried out as he shifted his weight. His palm moved slowly, oh so slowly over my clit. It was barely motion. But every agonizing second sent another streak of desire across my nerves.

"Ahh!"

His fingers moved in my mouth, sliding out. Instinct took me over, and I sucked. I sucked his fingers hard, the sweet icing melting on my tongue. He pushed his fingers back in, choking me, and I coughed, sucking harder, sucking more.

His palm eased up against me, leaving me aching for more. I arched my back to try and press against him, but he shoved my leg back with his.

"Lacey, you're not in charge here."

His words came hot against my skin, and I moaned with his fingers in my mouth.

His palm pressed against me again. *Oh Lord! Oh heaven!* The lights in the gallery seemed to flicker as my eyelashes fluttered. He moved his hand and the friction tore through me like thunder.

"If I want you to come, you will come. Understood?"

I no longer possessed my senses to be able to respond. Instead I moaned and leaned my head back against the wall. I closed my eyes, but his fingers made bright sparks fly across my vision in the darkness.

"Understood? You are mine. You will do what I say. Yes?"

"Yes!"

Every part of me was trembling with desire, like a live wire pressed against my nerves.

And his voice, God, his voice in my ear, telling me what I should do.

"Bend your knees slightly."

I did, and his fingers curled up into me, holding me up. *Oh, the pressure! The sweet, terrible pressure!* I longed to let myself go completely, to let him hold me against the wall and do whatever he would, no matter what happened.

"Now rock forward slightly. Yes, that's it. Back and forth."

I gasped as he curled his fingers tight, thrusting them into me at a shallow angle. My body clenched around his hand, and I could feel myself rocking onto his palm.

He pressed me harder with it. I could feel his upper lip, slightly sweaty, at my temple. His body smelled like molten iron, a sharp edge to the scent that drove me wild. Primal. I had nothing left to think with. I was only my body, and my body was being played expertly by his strong experienced fingers.

"Mmmmm!"

His hand was curling back and forth, rocking into me just enough to send bolts of desire through my limbs. Them he pulled back, leaving me breathless and wanting.

"MMM!"

He thrust his fingers into my lips and I sucked at them greedily. I tasted the sweetness of the sugar icing and the saltiness of his skin. Heat radiated from his body and I swam in his warm scent. This was like nothing I'd ever experienced.

"That's it. Good girl. Every last bit. All the way."

I rocked my body against his hand, and he responded with the same rhythm that sent me moaning. I'd never been hotter or wetter, not even when I had dreams that made me wake in sweat-covered sheets.

"Lacey, come for me," he whispered. And, oh, my dear Lord, he sounded like he was on the same edge as I was, about to jump off.

51

"AHHH!"

I couldn't see his eyes when he pressed against me. Mine were clenched shut too tight. But when he curled his fingers tight I screamed and screamed and could not stop.

It was an orgasm, that I knew. But it bore no resemblance to any of the weak trembles of satisfaction I'd given myself. This orgasm made me shiver down to the bone, turning my muscles liquid.

"Oh, God. OhGodOhGodOhGod."

I slumped back against the wall. His fingers slid from my mouth, and I rasped at the air. The room seemed to have heated up twenty degrees.

When I opened my eyes, I saw the painting first.

KAGE. The green and gold swam in front of me, and then my eyes refocused onto his face. His eyes. He licked his fingers. The fingers that had been inside me. He smiled.

Who was I? Not the girl who walked in the door. That girl wouldn't have done anything so reckless. That girl wouldn't take orders from anyone.

But now, panting and sweaty, I waited for him to speak. Waited for him to tell me what happened next. He straightened up in front of me. He gave me one more look, from my bare feet to the top of my head. I ran my hand through my hair shakily, sure that it had gotten completely messed up.

"Perfect," he murmured. "Just perfect. You'll do quite well."

I pulled the hem down on my dress, adjusting it as far down as I could. He held out the shawl to me and I took it from him, my eyes dropping down. I turned to go, but his hand stopped me.

"Wait," he said.

"You said I could go."

"Don't you want your tip?"

I stared as he pulled a wallet from his pocket. It was black, sleek leather. Like a seal's skin. He riffled through a few hundred dollar bills and pulled them out. I gaped down at the bills. It was five of them. Five hundred dollars.

"A... a tip?"

"Yes. Thank you for delivering the cake. I enjoyed it immensely."

I choked back the lump in my throat. I didn't want to take the money. Well, I mean, I *did*, but it didn't feel right. I'd fucked up a cake and let him finger me—was that how this worked? There was another feeling inside of me, a feeling that made this seem wrong. For some stupid reason, I didn't want this to be the end of tonight.

I wanted more than money. I didn't want to be a whore.

At least he didn't take your virginity, Lacey. Take the money and go.

I reached out and took the money quickly. I didn't have any pockets, so I crumpled the bills into my sweaty palm. I didn't look at the money. I didn't look at the Kage painting. I didn't deserve to look at them.

"When will you be back tomorrow?"

"Tomorrow?"

I stared at him.

"Yes. Tomorrow. Lucas told me that I had you for the whole week."

Chapter Seven

"Tomorrow?" I repeated dumbly. "Who's Lucas?"

"Cute. The innocence thing, very cute. I wish I could keep you here longer tonight," Jake said, pacing back and forth in front of the art gallery. He looked like his thoughts were already somewhere else. "But unfortunately, I have some business that needs taking care of."

"I can't come tomorrow," I stuttered. I felt like I was making a mistake, but I couldn't just stroll back into his penthouse. There seemed to be some kind of mixup. Lucas, whoever he was, hadn't told me anything and he hadn't told Steph anything. I had zero idea what was going on.

His eye twitched at the corner, and for a brief moment I saw him look at me with a flicker of anger. It terrified me. His gaze was so intense that I wanted to blurt out that I would come tomorrow even though I couldn't, I really couldn't.

"Lucas said you were a gift for the whole week. I'd like you here by eight in the morning sharp. You'll make my breakfast and—"

"Hold on."

I raised one of my hands in the air, still clutching the bills in the other hand.

"Hold on one second." Now I was getting my breath back, and my senses back. I could tell that there was something I was missing.

"What is it?" he snapped in irritation. "Don't tell me you didn't expect this. Lucas said—"

"I don't know who Lucas is," I interrupted.

"Of course you do. He's the one who sent you."

"I'm a friend of the baker's," I said carefully, being deliberate and calm with my words. "She told me to deliver—"

"Stop playing games," he said.

"I'm not!" Now adrenaline was pumping through my system. I wasn't about to let him yell at me for what was obviously a mix-up on someone else's part. "I don't know what you're talking about, asking me to come back tomor—"

"I'm not asking. I'm telling."

"Telling?"

"It's an order. Do you understand that?"

"I don't take orders from strange men."

"You will come tomorrow morning. You will not be late—"

"I won't be here at all tomorrow unless you tell me what the hell is going on," I said, crossing my arms. His irritation made every muscle of mine tense. He stood like a coiled snake, motionless, waiting to strike.

"Listen," he said, striding over in front of me. He pointed a finger in my face. "You're my gift, and I'll do with you as I like."

"I'm not a gift!"

That made him stop. His mouth opened, and then closed again. He seemed to be thinking. When he spoke again, his voice was slower. Calmer.

"What do you mean, you're not a gift?" he asked.

56

"Exactly that. I don't know who Lucas is, or what you're talking about, I was just here to bring up the cake—"

A knock on the door took both of our attention. I said "Come in!" at the same time as Jake said "Stay out!"

"Excuse me, Mr. Carville?"

The tuxedoed man stood in the doorway. It was the same one who had taken the girls once we'd gotten off of the elevator.

"This isn't the time, Stephen—"

"Your present from Mr. Black is here."

From the look on Jake's face and the deathly whiteness of his skin, Mr. Black was the man named Lucas. And things were about to get interesting.

***

"See?" I said. "Now do you believe me?"

Jake shot a scornful glare at me.

"Come in, Sophia," the tuxedoed man said. He tugged at a leash and through the door came my arch-nemesis from the elevator, the supermodel Blondie. Her eyes widened slightly in surprise when she saw me, then narrowed in anger.

"A gift for you, Mr. Carville. From Mr. Black. He sends his well wishes."

Blondie wasn't looking at me at all anymore. She'd turned her head away from me the instant she'd recognized me. Instead, she bent down on her knees on the carpet and laid her hands palm-down in front of her

"I'm here to serve you, master," she said.

I couldn't help it. I burst out laughing. It was just so... melodramatic. So cinematically hilarious. Snortfuls of laughter came from behind my hand as I clapped it over my mouth.

"I'm sorry," I murmured, as the tuxedoed man stared agape at me. "Really. I'm sorry."

Jake stepped toward the girl, and took the leash from the waiter.

Seriously? What was he going to do? For a split second, I actually felt jealous of her. Remembering the way he'd touched me made my skin grow hot.

He tugged at the leash and she stood up. She was perfectly balanced on her high stiletto heels. Despite my jealousy, part of me wanted to ask her for lessons on how to stand in those things.

"You're my gift?" Jake asked. He scrutinized her, walking around to her side and examining her profile.

"I will do whatever you want, master."

My heart was beginning to drop in my chest. Now he would kick me out. Now he would ask for his money back and throw me out on the curb like the street trash I was.

But instead, his eyes flickered up and down the blonde beauty. I took her in as I stood alongside him, seeing her with his eyes. The eyes of a man with desire pumping through his veins.

The perfect legs, smoothly shaved with no nicks. The perfect dress, hanging off of her hipbones. The perfect hair, not a flyaway in sight. She was beautiful, so perfect that it made me shrink back, ashamed to be a woman standing near her. The comparison would have been awful.

Then Jake reached out and unclasped her collar. He tossed it onto the floor.

"Master?" She looked confused. I noticed a crease at the corners of her perfectly mascaraed eyes.

"Get her out of here."

"Mr. Carville?" The tuxedoed man looked just as confused as I felt.

"Tell Lucas thank you, but her services won't be needed. I've found someone else."

"What? Her? Why?" the blonde supermodel interrupted.

He turned to her with a sharp fierceness in his eyes that stopped her cold. When he spoke, each word came with a punctuated stop.

"Because I... don't... want... you."

It's stupid, but my heart swelled with pride. He rejected her, the blond bimbo. He didn't want her. he wanted...

Oh God, he wanted me.

The tuxedoed man picked up the collar hurriedly and took the blonde girl by the arm. He flashed me a dirty look, like I'd fucked up his whole life. I smiled.

She walked out the door with as much dignity as she could. I gave her credit for that, at least. She was willing to bend to her knees and call someone Master, but at least she walked out tall in her high heels.

Then Jake turned to face me, and I felt my cheeks burn.

I was no better than her. Worse, maybe. Right then and there I would have done anything he wanted. Sucked his fingers, came all over him, I would have sunk to my knees in front of him like a goddamn pet. Just for the way he looked at me with desire in his eyes.

Was that terrible? *He chose me.*

"So you weren't my gift."

"It appears that way," I said.

I was trying to be funny, but it's hard to be funny when your voice is trembling so much you can hardly breathe.

"This was a misunderstanding," he said.

I frowned. He was polite. Too polite.

"It appears that way," I said again.

I didn't want this man. I wanted the Jake who had shoved me against a wall and made me come so hard I couldn't see straight. But now, Jake didn't even touch me as he moved by.

"But you enjoyed it?"

He looked at me from under lidded eyes.

"Enjoyed it?"

"What I did with you."

My core ached at his words, but I pressed my lips together and answered as smoothly as possible.

"I can take care of myself. I would have stopped you if…"

The hint of a smile appeared at the corner of his mouth. It cut off my words and made me sputter.

"If… That is…"

"Excellent," he said, cutting me off with one wave of his hand. "Then we understand each other."

Understand him? I doubted anyone understood Jake Carville. It was only sheer dumb luck that I had come into contact with him, and in a weird way, he had let me see more to him than probably most people would ever see. Those who weren't escorts, that is.

We were alone together again. Just him, me, and the artwork. I breathed in deeply. There was probably still time for me to get to work. Probably.

But I didn't want to leave him. The way he looked at me sent spasms of heat through my body. Echoes of the best orgasm I'd ever had. My first orgasm with a guy. If I didn't have work, I'd want to stay here forever.

"You should go home," he said, as though he had read my thoughts. "Tomorrow. Eight sharp. Or have I made a mistake in sending my gift away?"

I shook my head. The lump in my throat tasted like bitter chocolate, the sweet taste hidden inside if only I could get past the darkness. I would come back, I knew it. Even if I had to bribe Andy to take my shift at the restaurant, or beg my boss for a sick day. Even if I had to get Steph to loan me another dress. There was something about him that had an irresistible draw to me.

"I'll be here," I managed to choke out.

"Excellent. I'll see you tomorrow morning. Get a good night's rest."

"Okay. You, too. I mean, I'll see you too."

I backed away from the gallery. Away from Jake Carville. He followed me to the door and I picked up my heels in one hand. I wasn't about to stumble away from this man.

"Lacey?"

"Hm?"

The way he stared at me turned my skin into gooseflesh. His features looked darker staring out at me from the nearly-closed doorway.

"Tonight was an exception. I broke my own rules. That will not happen again. From now on, you are not allowed to disobey me at all. Understood?"

My tongue went dry as I thought about the orders he'd given me tonight, and what he might tell me to do tomorrow.

Chapter Eight

All of my emotions ran through me in a whirlwind as I strode away from Jake Carville. I clutched five hundred dollars in one hand and my pair of high heels in the other. I felt dizzy.

I glanced at the time as I got into the elevator. It was nearly nine o'clock. Shit. I was going to be late for my second job. I had five minutes. Steph's place was already five minutes away, and the bar was in the opposite direction. By the time I changed—

I couldn't change. I would have to sprint to my new job in these clothes and pray that they didn't care. Heck, maybe they'd be all about skimpy dresses. When I'd gone in to interview, the place looked seedy as a strip club.

The elevator plunged down, and I watched the lights of the city rise up around me. Rain pattered softly on the glass, and I realized that I would be running through the rain. The terror I'd felt on the way up was eclipsed by the terror I felt about losing my second job if I was late.

No. I wouldn't be late. I wouldn't.

I was racing so fast out of the building, I ran straight into Steph.

"Lacey, what's going on? I was waiting for you, and then the cakes came out, and you still weren't there, and it started to rain and I thought gosh, you don't have an umbrella, I'd better come and see—"

"No time to talk," I said, striding quickly down the sidewalk. Steph followed me, unsuccessfully dodging the mobs of people walking by. Her yellow-polka-dotted umbrella smacked a gutter, and she winced. "Come on! We have to run."

"Run?"

"I'm going to be late! Come on!"

"But your clothes are at my place—"

"Come on!"

We were a sight, the two of us. Steph had on a flour-stained apron over a cute pink flowered dress and white Keds, and a gust sent her umbrella inside out as she tried to keep up with me.

And me? I was trying not to step on any used needles or piles of dog shit, because there was no way I could run in heels, and no way I was going to be on time without running. It was disgusting, but hey, life was disgusting sometimes and you just had to make the best of it. As my mom always said, daisies grow prettier in horse shit.

The chilly November air tore at my throat as I inhaled and exhaled. My ears stung with the cold. There was a wind coming directly down through Seventh, and we were running against it, making it even colder.

My boobs flapped up and down as I ran. Oh, the curse of being well-endowed. I pressed one arm across my chest to try and keep them from flying everywhere. Huffing and puffing, I threw myself into one last sprint down the block and stopped at the corner.

"Okay. Okay," I said, breathing hard. Steph came running up behind me, slowing to a panting stop.

"My heart… is going to burst," she gasped. "Oh God. Oh God."

"The bar…it's right around the corner…next to the flower shop…" I said, rasping for breath in between talking. "How do I look?"

"I don't know," Steph groaned. "All I can see are black dots in front of my eyes."

"Are you okay?"

"Oh, God, I haven't run that many blocks since fifth grade."

"Okay, but seriously, Steph, concentrate now. How do I look?"

"You look… you look sexy," Steph wheezed. "Who's your makeup artist?"

"Am I okay to bartend, you think?"

"Are you going to take that shawl off?"

I scowled. "Come on."

"I'm coming with you? On your first shift? Isn't that weird?" Steph asked. "Like helicopter moms, you know. Would I be a *helicopter best friend*?"

"*We have to talk*," I said, looking at her meaningfully.

"Oh," Steph said, understanding dawning on her face. "Oh! Did he like the cake?"

I opened my mouth and then shut it. I took another breath through pursed lips.

"Sure. You… could say that."

***

I walked into the bar and immediately knew that I was dressed completely wrong.

Steph came up beside me and whistled a low whistle.

"Wow. You sure know where to pick places of employment, Lacey."

I should have come here on a weekend to check the place out, I know. But I hadn't. And now I was surrounded by a bunch of tattooed drunk dudes looking up and down at the two girls who were quite obviously new to this place.

"Be cool," I said. "I'll slip behind the bar and it'll be fine."

"That guy has a metal stud coming out of his forehead. His forehead! What is he, some kind of punk unicorn?"

"Shh, Steph!"

"Hey! Are you Lacey?"

A red-haired bearded guy wearing a flannel shirt emerged from the crowd of people. I exhaled in relief.

"New girl?" he asked.

"You're Casper, right?"

"Casper? Like the ghost?" Steph said.

"I'm sure he's *never* heard that one before, Steph," I said, rolling my eyes.

"Like the ghost, you got it," said Casper, who didn't seem to care one way or the other. His teeth flashed white from behind his red, bushy beard.

"So I'm ready to get started!" I said, trying to mask my nervousness as excitement. I was still recovering from the adrenaline rush of our sprint.

"Who's your friend?"

"This is Steph," I said.

"Like the princess?"

"What princess?" she asked.

"Princess Stephanie. The princess of Monaco," Casper said.

"I think you just made that country up."

"What? No, for real. Here, I'll show you." He pulled out his phone.

"Oh, come on," Steph said, pouting and fluttering her lashes. "Can't a girl flirt nowadays without being called out on her facts?"

"Ugh, quit it, Steph," I said, pushing past her. "Come on, Casper, show me the ropes."

"Make me an Old Fashioned when you get a chance!" Steph cried out from behind us. Caspar nearly knocked his head off nodding to her that he'd heard. I saw him slick one hand through his coppery hair and check it in the mirror as we went back around the bar.

Casper and I slid behind the bar as easily as if we'd been working together for years. I took beer orders from two guys who had been waiting, pouring both drafts at the same time. As I slid them over the bartop, he nodded appreciatively.

"Good head," he said, giving me a wink. "That's the most important part of this job."

"Let's hope I get a raise soon, then," I said, winking back.

Steph waited impatiently for me to get a moment to myself. I was impatient too—I couldn't wait to tell her everything that had happened—but this was a job, and I was going to do it right my first day. Fortunately, the other bartender was pretty cool about everything.

Casper showed me the bar pretty quickly—it was a standard setup, albeit a bit more crowded than I was used to. I'd tended bar before, so it only took a few minutes for him to realize that I would be able to handle the small mob with no problem.

"As long as you're my bouncer," I said.

"You got it. Oh, and let me show you something," he said.

He bent away from the crowd for a moment and motioned me down. I crouched next to him.

"This is the rubber floor mat," he said, pointing to our feet.

I frowned.

"A floor mat? Really? Is this why you made me crouch down?"

"Uh, no. It's… it's about your friend."

"About Steph?"

Casper looked at me with hope flickering in his eyes.

"Was she really flirting with me?"

Chapter Nine

As soon as the bar cleared out a bit, Steph and I were able to talk. I told her everything. Well, everything except for the part where I smashed her cake. I kind of left that part out.

"So a billionaire is in *love* with you?"

"Shh, no."

"But he wants you to come back tomorrow?"

"That doesn't mean he's in love with me, Steph. That means he wants to see me again."

"Immediately. He wants to see you again *immediately*. And for the whole week? What does that mean?"

"I don't know," I said.

"Oh my God, Lacey, you don't think he's going to take you prisoner as a sex slave and keep you locked in his dungeon?" Steph's eyes were wide.

"I don't think penthouses have dungeons."

"Penthouses have everything. I bet he has a dungeon where he locks up all of his girls with collars! And whips them and—"

"Excuse me, could I get the Ballast brew?"

"Sure," I said. I poured the drink and leaned back to Steph.

"So do you think I should go?" I said.

"What? Of *course* you should go!"

"But you just said it was dangerous. That he would lock me up as a sex slave—"

"Well, yeah, *maybe*. Or maybe he'll fall in love with you and want to marry you and then I could make the cake for your wedding and it would be perfect!"

I blinked.

"Okay, Steph, you are totally useless."

"I'm enthusiastic."

"Useless and enthusiastic."

"You're welcome," she said. "Promise me you'll let me be the godmother to your billionaire babies."

"I promise."

"Pinky swear?"

We put our arms across the bartop and I pinky swore.

"And if you go missing for a week, I promise to call the police and tell them you've been abducted as a sex slave by a sexy billionaire."

"Just don't call them until after the week's up, okay?"

"Yes, ma'am! I'll tell them exactly that."

"I think they'd lock you up in the looney bin, Steph."

"That's princess Steph to you," she said, raising her cocktail and tipping it my direction before quaffing the last sip. "And you'll be billionairess Lacey!"

"You'd better go eat a cupcake to soak up some of that gin in your system."

"It's like tiramisu, but tastier. And drunker."

"Exactly."

I saw Andy at the door and waved to him.

"Your brother's here."

"Oh, good," Steph said, slurring a bit. "He can have a cupcake too."

Andy came over and helped Steph up off of her stool. They looked nothing alike at first—he was a scrawny bean pole compared to Steph, long and lean—but both of their eyes flashed the same golden-brown laughter.

"Thanks for coming to pick me up, little bro!" she said.

"No problem," Andy said, checking out Casper's back side as he bent over the ice bin. Great, they could fight over Casper between the two of them.

"This is where you're working now, Lace?" Andy asked.

"Sure is," I said.

"Nice place. Okay, let's go back. You ready to go back, Teph?"

Steph nodded and I leaned across the bar to give her a hug.

"Goodnight, princess Steph," I said.

"Goodnight, billionairess Lacey!"

***

After Steph left, there wasn't much to do. People came in, people came out, and the hours ticked by slowly. Casper sat on the side of the bar reading a comic book.

Soon, it was four in the morning and time to close up. I cleaned down all the tables and started mopping the back. Casper hauled the trash out to the alley.

"Bathrooms need to be cleaned," he said.

"Already did it," I replied.

"Are you for real?"

He wrapped his arms around me in a friendly drunken bear hug.

"You bring cute girls to the bar and clean the bathrooms without having to be yelled at. You're an angel. Can you work tomorrow night?"

"Tomorrow? Oh, um. I'm not sure."

Normally I would be jumping at the chance for an extra day of tips, but Jake Carville wanted me back at his place tomorrow, and I had no idea how long I'd be there. The mere thought of those luscious lips and dazzling emerald eyes made me flush. I hoped he would keep me there a while. I hoped—

"Can I text you later this morning and let you know?" I asked.

"Sure. No problem if not, but working with you sure makes the night go by easier," Casper said.

"Thanks." I grinned. It was good to be useful, even if useful only paid minimum wage plus tips.

I went out to the alley with the last bag of recycling.

A black SUV pulled into the alley. The headlights were on high, and as the car swung in, the light blinded me. I held my hand up.

"Hey, come on," I said, annoyed. It was late, and I was tired, and this alley didn't even go through to the next street. I swung the bag up into the recycling bin. Then I heard the car door open.

Then I heard another car door open.

Instinct made me stop. Fear made me drop the second bag. Before my mind even knew it, my body was preparing for flight.

As soon as I saw the silhouette of a man step out in front of the lights, I turned to run. The men from the car sprinted toward me at full speed.

My heel caught in a crack and I cried out as I fell. I didn't even hit the ground. Four strong arms caught me and pulled me back. The men were wearing all black, with ski masks covering their faces. I wrenched away but they were too big. I was helpless in their grasp.

"Help!" I shouted, but they were already pulling me into the back of the SUV. One man held me tight in his arms. Another hand covered my mouth and muffled my screams. I kicked out at the driver.

"Cut it out," the driver said. "Jesus, how did he ever find this one?"

"Dunno. Here, put this over her face. That should do it."

I squealed as a hand clapped a handkerchief over my nose and mouth. I writhed from one side to the other, trying not to breathe. Soon, though, the ache for oxygen was so strong that I couldn't help myself.

I gasped. There was a slight smell of lemon, and then the world around me blurred. I slumped back. Two men, both with black ski masks, leaned over and watched. I reached up, but my arm didn't move.

"What—what did you—" My words were slow and heavy.

They were talking, but none of the words made sense to me. My body was getting heavier, heavier. A

73

seatbelt slid across my chest. I stared down at it, the dizziness overtaking me. Seatbelts made you safe. Was I safe?

"Safe," I mumbled. That was the last word I remember saying before I slipped into darkness.

Chapter Ten

When I came to, I was blindfolded.

I was so dizzy that for a moment, I couldn't tell if I was standing up or lying down. I breathed in slowly, then out. Whatever it was that had knocked me out, it had knocked me out completely. I didn't remember anything after being put in the car by those men.

The men. Where were they? My heart began to pound. No. I had to stay calm. I had to figure my way out of this. First thing, I had to stop being so dizzy and figure out where I was.

Okay. I was lying on my back. On a bed? It felt like I was on a bed. There was a hint of light coming in through the folds of the fabric over my eyes, but only a hint. I couldn't make out any details, only smudges of light.

I tried to pull my hands down, but they caught on something. I tugged, but they wouldn't move. They had tied ropes around my wrists. No. Handcuffs. Lined with something.

My ankles, too. I still had Steph's little black dress on, but I could feel the hem riding up my thigh.

"Lacey."

I twisted in shock at the whisper. My heart skipped a beat and began to hopscotch against the skin of my chest.

It was him.

It had to be. He knew my name.

Jake?

I tried to speak, but there was a piece of silk cloth over my mouth. A gag, tied tight. I moaned behind the fabric.

"I told you that I wouldn't accept any disobedience."

"Mmm!" I shook my head, slowly but firmly. *I hadn't disobeyed!*

"I told you to go home and get a good night's sleep," Jake said. "And what did you do? You were out until after four o'clock in the morning."

Holy crap, was he serious? Was he going to punish me for going to *work*? What kind of a sick fuck was he, anyway?

My arms and legs yanked at their knots, but I could tell by their tightness that I wasn't going anywhere.

"Mmm!"

He said nothing as I writhed against the ropes that were binding me. My brain was still fuzzy, or maybe that was the effect of the blindfold. Was this a dream?

I breathed hard against the gag. In the dark, I could feel my body tensing bit by bit as I woke up from whatever crazy sedative they'd given me.

It had been a while since he spoke. When his voice came, it was from the bottom of the bed. I breathed in. *Orient yourself.*

"I want you to know that I'm not going to harm you, Lacey. There's no need to be afraid."

I wanted to scream back at him. I wanted to thrash around. But what would any of that accomplish?

That was what he wanted. I wasn't going to give him the satisfaction. I lay there completely still. Listening.

Waiting.

His footsteps came around the bed. The mattress was padded and I could barely hear the mattress give under his weight as he sat next to me.

I swallowed hard. Fabric brushed my arm. His jacket, maybe.

He was sitting there. Sitting next to me. Despite myself, my body began to react to his nearness with a heat that spread quickly down through my chest, down to my thighs and between. He was sitting right there next to me, and I couldn't stand the blindfold.

"You're an artist, yes, Lacey?"

I didn't move. I didn't nod. I wasn't playing his game, whatever it was.

"An artist. And now I've blinded you. I wonder if this will be harder."

Harder to do what?

"You're behaving much better now, Lacey," Jake whispered. "Even if you can't answer me. I understand that this is going to be more difficult. But I think you'll enjoy this by the end."

What? What was going to be difficult?

His hand touched my stomach and I cried out from behind the gag. His hand rested, simply rested on my stomach. His fingers were warm through the fabric of my dress.

This touch was all he needed to tell me that I was his. With it, he proved my vulnerability. I couldn't slap his hand away, couldn't wrench out of the ropes that tied all of my limbs back.

He had me there, completely his, unable to get away.

My breaths began to come faster.

In my terror there was a strange fascination. Jake Carville didn't strike me as the type of man who would harm me. Weird, I know, since I was tied to his bed. But the way he'd spoken to me, the gentle spark of desire in his eyes—these things made me want to trust him.

Even now, in the way he spoke, there was a cool certainty to his words that gave me pause.

He spoke to me as though he knew already that I was going to like whatever he did. God save me, I was curious. So curious. I wasn't some prude. Sure, I was a virgin, but it wasn't like that was on purpose. Guys mostly saw me as friends, and that was as far as it went.

In Jake's eyes, though, there was more. Much more. And it scared me, yes. I was lying blindfolded on a bed, my hands and ankles tied. It scared me. And it made me wonder.

His hand moved down my stomach. Slowly, but not inching. He was going to take what he wanted. I could feel myself throbbing. Hot. Wet. Did I want it? God, I did. My body did, and it was going to drag my mind along for the ride no matter what.

I was tied down, wasn't I? I was helpless. I couldn't do anything, and I found myself wanting to give in. I wanted to let my body respond willingly to him, the way it wanted to instinctively.

My lips trembled. I waited in the dark.

His fingers slid to my hip, his one hand caressing the slow curves of my body. He stopped at the hem of my dress. His fingers hovered, grazing my skin there.

Then he shifted his weight on the bed. I felt the motion against my leg, and then there was another hand on my body. He gripped both of my hips, his thumbs caressing the shape of my hipbone.

He must have bent forward, because I felt his weight come to bear on his hands. The pressure pinned my hips down against the bed. Then—

His breath. Oh God, his mouth is right there, right there on top of me, breathing on me. My body spasmed and I kept myself from arching up against his face. It was an effort not to cry out with the ache.

Behind the gag, my lips parted slightly. I let my tongue come forward and push against the silk fabric binding my mouth. The air was dark, damp, and so hot that I felt every inch of my skin begin to itch with heat.

His lips pressed against me through the fabric. He held his mouth there, over my most sensitive part, simply breathing. The coolness of his inhale. The excruciating heat of his exhale. I twitched, but his hands were strong. They held me down easily.

He murmured something, his lips moving so softly that I nearly died from the brushing glances against my aching body.

The physical thrill of his nearness made me dizzy. Eventually, though, his words came together and I could hear what he was saying.

"Lacey," he murmured. "Lacey."

My name, over and over again. His voice hummed my name, rolling off of his tongue as softly as silk. I couldn't hold back a low moan.

His hands, both of them, slid under the hem of my dress. His fingers pulled the fabric up so that I was naked except for the pair of panties I'd been wearing all night. They were soaked with the juices of my desire.

When he pulled my dress up, I tensed. Every muscle in my body went rigid. I had no idea what he was doing, and I didn't want to mess it up, and God, oh God, I wanted to see him and see his eyes and know that it was him out there, him touching me. Him taking my virginity and giving something back.

He hadn't even kissed me yet.

Jake paused, reading my hesitation. Then he reached up. His fingers loosened the gag around my mouth. I licked my lips, breathing in air that couldn't cool me enough.

Maybe I should have cried out for help. I didn't. I couldn't.

"Jake?" I asked. My voice was tremulous, but it seemed louder. Perhaps it was the blindfold that made it sound like I was speaking loudly in whatever room I was in.

"Lacey?"

"What—what are you—"

"Do you need me to stop?"

"What?"

"Tell me now if you can't go on. If you want me to stop. I don't... I don't normally ask. But you aren't a normal employee. So tell me now. Speak up if you don't want this. If you say so, I'll send you back out with my men and you'll never see me again."

My body recoiled at the idea of stopping. I ached for him, needed more, needed it now. And I was so curious. About him, about who he was. I didn't want to stop. No. Crazy as it sounds, I wanted this.

He waited for me for a second. Then he moved to put the gag back over my mouth.

"Wait!" I cried out.

"You want me to stop?"

"No! I just—what are you going to do to me?"

"What am I going to do to you?" His voice had a smile in it, although I couldn't see anything.

"Yes," I said timorously. My fingers clutched and released the ropes that were binding my hands to the bedposts.

"Then you've decided to stay? You don't want me to stop?" Jake asked. I could hear a hint of teasing in his voice, a lilt that made me melt inside.

I shook my head. I knew what my answer was.

A new fear trembled through my heart. A fear of the unknown.

I'd come willingly into the dark forest, and now I would see what wild things lived there.

***

"No," I said, feeling the echoes of the weight of my decision reverberate into the depths of my mind. "I want to stay."

"Excellent," Jake said, pulling the gag back over my mouth. I tried to speak, but he tightened the knot quickly.

"Verbal contract, signed contract, payment already accepted for services. Now that we've got those formalities out of the way…"

His hands ran down my body, squeezing firmly. I writhed at his touch, now more demanding than before. My hands pulled at the ropes that bound me.

He cupped my breast and squeezed, sending a shock of pain through my body. I squealed.

"What am I going to do with you? Lacey. Oh, Lacey. What *won't* I do with you?"

His fingers pinched and twisted my nipples. I screamed behind the gag at the same time as I throbbed for him. Every touch of his, even the rough ones, sent aches of desire through my core.

Especially the rough ones.

"I'm going to do all of the things I wanted to do to you last night."

His hands were everywhere, touching, pinching, kneading my muscles. He squeezed my ass tight, then kneaded it with his strong fingers. My muscles went from tense to relaxed and back in a split second. I didn't know where he would touch me next, but he was touching everywhere around me, everywhere but where I wanted it the most.

"I'm going to take you to the edge of darkness, my Lacey. My little artist. You'll see the colors I can paint with my touch."

At that, he twisted my nipple, then rolled it with his thumb. And I saw, I saw what he was talking about. Red and white flashes of light pulsed behind my eyes with the pain.

In the darkness, there was still color.

His hands reached up, then, to the collar of my dress. He'd already taken off the shawl, and now his hands pulled my large breasts out from my bra, exposing them. His hands rolled them heavy in his palms, and he squeezed them, pressing them together and then rolling them apart.

He was using me. His hands told me that they would do what they wanted. They would pull and yank and wrench and I could do nothing. Nothing. The collar of the dress stretched at my neck. I winced as the fabric dug into my skin.

"Uncomfortable?"

He could sense my every reaction. Now, though, he took hold of the dress in the front. I felt a sharp yank and heard a loud tearing sound. I whimpered aloud. He had ripped the dress straight down the middle, ripped it in two.

That was Steph's dress, I thought numbly, before his hands brought my attention back to my nipples. Despite his roughness—

—because of it, because of the roughness, my body screamed—

—despite his roughness, my breasts were tight and aching for more pressure.

His thumbs rolled over the sensitive nubs, and I yelped as I felt his mouth come down on my nipple. Immediately my body was aflame, and I couldn't help squirming under his touch, even as he continued to pinch and squeeze my other breast with his hand.

His tongue traced circles around my tender nipple. I felt myself aching and I needed him. Needed him to suck me, needed him to lick me. What he was doing to my nipple, I felt between my thighs.

I was already so close to orgasm, but the sharp jolts of pain he kept giving me tore me back from the edge. My breath was heavy and I was ready to arch against him to satisfy myself, when suddenly he stopped.

He pulled back. His hands disappeared from my body. His warmth disappeared. I could feel him shifting away from me, pulling back. I yanked on the handcuffs but they held me fast.

My entire body ached for him to return. I needed it. Needed the pressure, needed his rough hands to thrust inside me and take me over the edge. I was so close, God, *so close!*

My face contorted along with my body. Why was he doing this? What had I done?

Again, he read my mind. Or not my mind, but my body. The confusion and pain and longing all at once. Maybe I was not the first girl he'd done this too. But his calm voice did nothing to ease the hot desire pulsing through my bloodstream.

No. When he spoke, desire mixed with fear. Not because he sounded angry, but because he didn't.

"My dear," he said, each word clipped and measured, "You have disobeyed a direct order. You disobeyed *me*. That is not a sign of respect."

He paused, waiting, I think, for the realization to sink in. He wasn't waiting because he didn't know I ached for him. He knew. He wanted me to ache for him. To ache and ache, and never get relief. A cry strangled in my throat.

"You lied to me, my dear Lacey. And now I'm going to punish you."

***

HIS GIFT: PART TWO

A DARK BILLIONAIRE ROMANCE

Chapter One

I'm going to punish you.

Jake said it so calmly that I almost couldn't understand the words. Then the full meaning hit me, and my chest tensed.

Blindfolded, handcuffed, gagged, completely undone with desire, I'd decided to stay. My curiosity had already decided that for me. But that one word—*punish*—filled me with dread.

His hands were gone. They left an absence on my body that ached like a bruise.

"Lacey, you beautiful girl. You beautiful, silly girl. You're the innocent gift I was hoping for. That other girl, she wouldn't have done anyway. But you—"

Even though I was blinded by the dark silk fabric, I could feel his weight as he leaned over me, his hands pressed on either side of me against the sheets. In my mind, I could see his green eyes, dazzling and fierce.

I tugged with one arm, then the other. Both wrists, cuffed on either side of me. I couldn't go anywhere. I couldn't even touch him unless he touched me.

"You are something special, Lacey. As unhappy as I am about your lying to me—"

"Mmm!" I cried out from behind the gag.

Jake's knees were between my thighs and the very thought of it made me sick with want. I had never had such an ache, as though my body had been hollowed out. I shook my head back and forth.

"Yes, you lied. But as unhappy as I am about your lying, I think that you did it on purpose."

One of his hands touched my breast, and God help me, my body arched into him. I needed him. I needed that pressure. Needed that release.

"Yes, you did it on purpose so that I would have to punish you."

I moaned. He had brought me to the brink of orgasm and left me waiting, hanging off of the edge and not being able to fall.

My hands were tied. So were my feet. I struggled, but only for a moment longer. Was I giving him what he wanted? It didn't matter.

He would take what he wanted.

I moaned again.

His hand brushed down my chest. The back of his fingers grazed my exposed breast, sending electric thrills through my limbs.

"Ohh," I moaned behind the gag. I was wet, so wet. Last night he had touched me and made me come. But now...

"I said I wouldn't harm you. And I won't. But that doesn't mean it won't hurt. Do you understand?"

I blinked behind the fabric of the blindfold.

I didn't understand.

My bra and panties were still on, albeit in a state of wild disarray, and he made no motion to take them off. Instead, he slid his hand over my panties, fondling me through the fabric.

Oh God. I couldn't imagine that this was how it was with every man. No other man had ever made me burn so hot with a single look. It wasn't only his fingers that were sending me into spasms of want. It was the fact that it was *him*.

Jake Carville, a man I knew almost nothing about. I knew only that he was rich—

—*you knew that his fingers were long and hard, and probably so was his*—

rich, yes, rich and powerful, but the greatest power he had was this, the power to make my body sing under his fingertips.

Before, he'd yanked down my bra so that my breasts were exposed. I could feel the chill of the air and the warmth of his breath. His hair brushed against my collarbone as he lowered his head to my chest.

I would have screamed if I hadn't been gagged. I screamed anyway, but it came out as little more than a gurgle behind the black silk fabric.

His tongue slipped down the line of my throat, leading down between my breasts. He turned his head there and rested his cheek against my chest.

Could he feel how fast my heart was beating? The quick throb of my pulse that beat through every vein of my body? It felt like the room was beating and all I could see was darkness.

A dark, beating air pressed hot against my face, and he pressed his fingers against me. I moaned, my hips bucking out to him, trying desperately to drain pleasure from his touch.

But no, he withdrew those long, terrible fingers and brought his hands up to my chest instead. He cupped my breasts in both of his hands. My first thought as he did so was that his hands must be so big to fit around me completely. Then he squeezed me, pressing a soft kiss against the space over my heart, and I didn't think anymore.

His hands caressed softly, but I didn't want him to be soft. I wanted him as he had been before. I wanted his hands to thrust roughly into me. I needed relief. I needed satisfaction.

Behind the gag I growled with need.

Hearing me, he smiled. I could feel the curl of his lips against my skin. He pinched my nipple slightly, teasing me. With the other hand he continued to massage my chest, kneading the soft, aching flesh.

"Lacey, my darling. My innocent," he whispered. I heard his voice swimming in the darkness, and I tossed my head from one side to the other. The pounding need inside of me was ready to swallow me whole. All I needed from him was one thrust. One finger inside me, one hand pressing against my swollen clit. God, I needed it.

Then he bent his head and sucked on my nipple. I swear, I almost came right then from the thought of his mouth on another one of my aching nubs. The thought of him doing what he was doing with his tongue—long, slow swirls—between my thighs. Oh, God, it was almost enough.

Almost.

Jake paused for a moment, his teeth grazing my nipple on top and bottom. I arched slightly, wanting him to suck harder. Even just a little harder, and I would be there. But no. His teeth slid lightly, teasing, torturing.

He slid his fingers down over my panties, brushing my swollen, aching nub so gently that I screamed with desire behind the gag. I couldn't distract myself; with the blindfold on, there was only *him*. He kissed me on the underside of my breast, his tongue lapping at the curve from my armpit to my sternum.

Light kisses, like a paintbrush dabbing airily at my skin. He kissed my shoulder, my arms, pressing these impossible soft lips against my wrist, retreating if I moaned.

He kissed me everywhere but where I needed him.

All the while, his fingers slid on both sides of my panties, teasing the hemline. I was soaking wet and God, I had never thought much about losing my virginity but at that moment I would have given it to anyone who promised a quick, hard finish.

Jake brushed against me and I whimpered, needy and stupid, whimpering like a little girl. I'd always been a tomboy, always been tough, but this was too much.

He brought me to the edge and then held me there, torturing me with the promise of another mind-blowing orgasm.

But relief never came.

I felt Jake's fingers retreat, and I nearly cried.

He took off my gag. The silk fabric dropped away from my mouth. I tried to speak, but my mouth was too dry. I coughed, my tongue screaming for moisture.

"Please," I rasped. "Please."

I never begged, but here I was, begging. He had turned me into a sputtering mess of emotion. I hated the way he toyed with me, but I needed him to do more.

"No," he said.

It was then that I understood. He wasn't going to take me. He wasn't going to have sex with me.

And that was the punishment.

Chapter Two

The cuffs around my wrists came off, Jake's fingers touching my wrists as he undid them. I had to struggle not to reach down and finish myself. My body pulsed with desire between my thighs.

Still blindfolded, I bit my lip and breathed like Steph had taught me when she had started her newest yoga class.

Breathe in. Feel everything around you. Feel your body.

Well, I felt my body, alright. My body was *burning.*

Breathe out. Relax.

My heart was racing, but I did my best to breathe slowly. Knowing that he was torturing me gave me strength to fight the deep urge that was burning at my core. I wouldn't let him beat me. This was a game of will, and I had willpower to last forever if I needed to.

God, I hoped I didn't need to.

"Don't move," Jake said, as if he needed to tell me. "Don't take off your blindfold."

"Where are we?" I whispered. I hadn't really been curious before. I'd supposed that I was on his bed, in his bedroom. But the way he spoke the order made me doubt it. Now curiosity tingled, and I licked my lips.

Breathe in. Breathe out.

His strong arms came around me and I felt him carry me. I couldn't make out anything from under the blindfold, and after a few steps I gave up, nuzzling my head against his strong chest. I tried not to think about the ache between my legs, about the way his lips had danced across all of my skin.

One door opened and closed, and then another. His arms set me down on another cushioned surface.

He took off the blindfold. Seeing his dazzling emerald eyes above me made me hate him and want him even more. He looked pleased with himself.

I looked around. We were in a bedroom for sure, this time. The decor matched the rest of the penthouse apartment that I'd seen. Plush carpet lined the floors, with thick braided rugs elaborately embroidered. More paintings, vintage oils framed in gold, hung on the walls.

This bed was covered in pillows that felt like down against my back. The bed itself was a four-post canopy, with rich oak posts at all its corners.

In my history classes in middle school, I remembered seeing a picture of fourteenth century Versailles. The palace that was so lavish it made the peasantry rise up and revolt. If Jake Carville had lived back then, I thought idly, he would most certainly have gone to the guillotine.

And outside of the bedroom window, I could see the rest of New York City, bright and shining in the night's darkness.

"Where are we?" I asked, the breath coming back to my lungs. Now that I had seen his expression, I certainly wasn't going to be touching myself, even though there was still a dull pulse of desire. I crossed my arms over my bra. My panties were soaked with desire and it was starting to cool now that he had stopped touching me. I shivered.

"This is a guest room in my apartment. You are my guest."

"Really? Do you kidnap all of your guests in dark alleys and tie them up blindfolded before torturing them?"

"No," he said, grinning slyly. "Only the ones I like best."

"Hrmph," I said. And yet my mind screamed at me. *Liked the best? He liked me. Jake Carville liked me. He--*

His hand reached out and for a moment I thought that this was the moment. He'd made me wait, but now he would take me. Take my virginity. My pulse began to beat harder.

But no. He was only reaching out to stroke my hair, tucking one strand behind my ear. It was an oddly touching gesture for someone who had spent the past hour denying me an orgasm.

"Well, Lacey? What do you think? Have I punished you enough?"

"Why are you punishing me?"

The question came to my lips before I knew it was there. My breaths came hard and fast. My body was twisting inside. I needed him to touch me, just a little more pressure, just a little—

"For your disobedience."

Breathe in. Breathe out.

"What disobedience?" I asked, trying not to sound too sarcastic.

"Staying out late. I told you to rest."

My jaw fell open. So much for not being sarcastic.

"Are you serious?"

"Of course," he said, frowning. His dark brows slanted over those piercing green eyes, but there was no humor in them. He wasn't teasing me. He wasn't joking.

"I had to *work*," I said, frowning right back at him.

"I ordered you to rest," he said. He emphasized the word *ordered*.

"And my landlord ordered me to pay rent. Sorry for not wanting to get evicted." My arms were already crossed, but if I could have crossed them again, I would have. Of all the jerk moves, this was absolutely the worst.

His eyes narrowed. Good. All of my arousal was quickly turning into anger. If I could just stay mad at him, I could calm my body down.

"If you aren't going to obey me for some idiot reason—"

"Not having money is an idiot reason?"

Jake's nostrils flared. I could tell that he wasn't used to being interrupted in the middle of a sentence. Well, too bad. If he didn't want me interrupting him, he shouldn't have had his henchmen grab me off the street like I was in some Liam Neeson movie.

Instead of yelling at me, though, he reached into his jacket and pulled out a checkbook.

"How much?"

"How much what?"

"How much is your rent?" he asked with concealed impatience, like I was asking him stupid questions. He was the one asking stupid questions, and if I didn't want him so badly I might have stormed off to find the elevator out of his gorgeous palace of an apartment.

Instead, I swallowed, breathed in and out, and answered his question.

"Six hundred." Six hundred for a closet that someone thought made a good studio apartment.

"That's it?"

"I guess my penthouse apartment is just a better deal than yours," I said, smirking sarcastically. "How much is *your* rent?"

Jake didn't answer. He wrote a check and set it down on the bed next to me. I stared down at it, then picked it up gingerly, holding it as though it had teeth. I read the number.

At first I thought he had heard me wrong.

"This is too much. Way too much," I said. "That's...uh...it's..." I tried to do the math in my head and failed horribly. I didn't do well with numbers, even when I wasn't burning at the groin with a hot billionaire sitting next to me in a silk-sheeted bed.

"It's a year's rent."

I stared at him dizzily. A year? A whole year?

"No more excuses. If I say rest, you rest. Understood?" He eyed me meaningfully.

"Why do you care so much about my good night's sleep?"

"I don't think you understand. I'm protecting my gift."

Whoa. I put the check down and lifted both hands in the air. This needed to stop.

"Okay, first? I'm not your gift. Lucas, whoever that is, didn't give me to you."

"I know that. The woman he'd picked out wasn't quite as nice of a gift as you."

"I'm not a gift."

"Sure you are," Jake said.

"Oh? Please. Explain that to me, if Lucas didn't give me to you."

"The universe gave you to me," he said, smiling.

Man, this guy was an arrogant ass. I put on a sarcastic smirk.

"Lucky you, that the universe would do you such a favor. Wow, the universe just plopped me down on your doorstep, didn't even leave a gift receipt or anything! You must just be the luckiest man in the world."

The smile on his face faltered. His eyes shaded with pain.

"I have been lucky in some ways," Jake said, his voice softer. "Not so much in others."

"You must be at least a little lucky. You've got this, don't you?" I looked out of his bedroom window where the bustle of New York City spread out in all directions. He had a beautiful home. Riches beyond imagining. He had everything. "Or are you a self-made man? Hard work, pulling yourself up by your own bootstraps—"

"No, you were right the first time. This was given to me."

He said it baldly, with no small amount of pain in his voice. Despite myself, I felt sorry for him. Ha! Sorry for a billionaire!

Still, the way he said it made me realize that I was being kind of a jerk to him. He was lavishing me with compliments. Heck, he'd given me a check for a year's worth of rent. I could at least play along a little bit. Now that I was calming down, I struggled to say something nice.

"It's beautiful either way," I said softly. "And hey, you could have spent all your money like those lottery winners who go broke. At least there's that."

Yes." He looked at me, and the pain dropped away from his face. He smiled again, a glint in his eye. "And now, I have you."

He bent down and licked me through my panties. My hands dropped to his head, meaning to pull him away, but I couldn't. Oh God, I couldn't. All of the terrible aches inside of me that I had been trying to calm down flamed right back up immediately. My fingers threaded through his dark hair as he lifted his head from between my legs.

"*Ahh*," I moaned. I pulled his head down only slightly with my hands, needing him but not wanting to admit it.

"Say it. Say you want me."

Breathe in. Breathe out. I wouldn't give him the satisfaction, not yet.

He licked me again, nuzzling softly. It wasn't enough. It wasn't nearly enough. I groaned.

"Alright. I want you. I want you! Jake—"

"Don't say my name." He stopped then, suddenly. I remembered what he'd told me before. He didn't like his name. Or maybe he just didn't like hearing it from the girls he brought up to his place. Either way, I didn't care. All I cared about was the aching pressure inside and his hard tongue against my most intimate places.

"Okay, okay, just please! Please, I want you. I can't stand it! Please let me come, oh God!"

"Good."

He sat up. I could have cried when I realized that he wasn't going to finish me off.

"No. Come on. Please. Please don't do this to me."

"Do what?" He was grinning again, teasing me with his eyes. Those gorgeous emerald eyes. I wanted to fall into his bed. My hands weren't tied, but I knew that no touch of mine could quench the thirst I had for only one man. For him.

Lord, I didn't even know what sex was like and I needed it.

"Do what?" I echoed at him breathlessly. "Do *what?*"

"I didn't do anything."

"You tied me up. You tortured me! What kind of man does that to a woman?"

"What kind of woman enjoys it?"

I stared at him, agog. Eventually, my tongue found the words for a response.

"Don't you dare blame me," I said.

"It's not about blame," he said. "I only want you to see in yourself what I see in you."

"Really? What do you see in me?"

For a moment he didn't answer, and my body itched. Not just with my unsatisfied desire, although that was part of it. When he looked at me, really looked at me, it seemed like he was looking too far down. Like he could see deep into me. Like he could know what I really wanted.

I flushed and turned my cheek to him. He reached out and placed a finger under my chin. He turned me back to face him.

"You're beautiful. Every part of you, every inch of smooth skin. Your curves. Your fingers. Your toes. You're innocent. But I see a loneliness in you, Lacey. Your worrying sends lines down your face. I see you reaching out without reaching out, asking without asking. Because you never want to ask for it, do you?"

I was quivering as he withdrew his finger from under my chin. I shook my head slowly.

"Don't."

"Do you think independence is about being alone? About being completely in control, all by yourself?" He smiled and arched his eyebrow at me. "You can't, you see. You can't be in control without someone there to control."

I narrowed my eyes.

"Is that all you want? Control?"

"No. Oh, no. Lacey. I want so much more."

The implication of those words set my body afire. I stared at him, not really understanding what he'd said. Well, except the part about being lonely. But that was true of anyone, wasn't it? Everybody was lonely sometimes.

"Well, you control me now," I said, trying to regain some of my confidence while boosting his.

"Do I?"

"You hold all the strings. Don't you?"

He ignored my question. Instead, he went to the closet and pulled out a robe.

"You're shivering," he said, laying the robe on the bed. It was white terrycloth.

I'd been shivering, but it wasn't the cold.

"I'm fine," I said, but I stood up and pulled the robe on. It reached all the way down and brushed over the tops of my feet.

For a brief moment, I was consumed with jealousy. What other girls did he have here? Were they tall, graceful supermodels? Did this robe fit them perfectly? Then he put a hand on my shoulder, and I brushed away the thought.

"Come with me," he said.

He went smoothly into the hallway and I followed behind. This was a different hallway than the one I'd been in before. Another part of the apartment, another floor maybe.

"Where are we going?"

"Don't talk anymore," he said gruffly.

He walked in front of me and I tried to keep up with his long strides. I tied the robe clumsily around my waist. If there were any servants in this part of the house, I didn't want to run into them half-naked.

"Is this the same floor as the party was on?" I asked, pausing briefly to check out a pastel painting on one of the walls. A Cezanne. Jesus, this guy was rich.

"Don't talk."

"But—"

Instead of telling me to shut up again, he opened a door to his right and stepped through into the room. I stepped in behind him, and I was struck dumb by what I saw.

Chapter Three

It was a studio. No, it was *the* studio. The art studio of my dreams, if I had ever imagined something as lavish as this.

One long window at the east end looked out over New York City. The sun was beginning to peek out from over the horizon. Pink and orange light shone in, bouncing off of the mirrored windows. From this room I could see why the sky had been getting lighter.

Sunrise. It seemed like it should have been longer. Last night I had left Jake and gone to work. Last night, after he had touched me.

The recent memory sent blood rushing again between my thighs. I ignored it and stepped further into the room.

Everything was white. All of the walls, the ceiling. The floor was smooth white. There weren't even any lines, although I would swear that it was tile under my bare feet.

And everywhere, stacked by the half dozen against each other, were canvases. Big canvases. Small canvases. Square and rectangular, in every proportion. They scattered across the room and propped against the walls.

Across from the window was another door. It was the only thing in the room that wasn't white, it seemed. It was wood, dark wood, with a padlock on the outside of it.

Turning slowly, I saw the table that was just to the side of the door. The cabinets were painted white as well, but I could imagine what was inside: brushes, paints. And more canvases, stacked like they weren't the most precious thing.

Blank canvases. All of them waiting, ready for paint. All of them yearning to be covered.

I breathed in through my teeth and let out the breath in a slow hiss. I had been tired at the end of my shift, and I'd been awake for hours since then. But this room sent a rush of adrenaline through me that made my fingers itch to work. Almost as much as my body itched to be scratched by Jake's own fingers.

I glanced back at him, waiting for an explanation. He gave me an order instead.

"Paint."

"What?"

I wanted to believe him, but I couldn't. I would have pinched myself, but it wouldn't have made any difference. This was a dream whether I was asleep or awake.

"You said you were an artist."

"I'm half-naked and—" I cut myself off before I could say *extremely aroused.*

He smiled, as though reading my thoughts.

"It's good. You have blood rushing through your system. You have emotions."

"Sure." I have emotions. Like total irritation. Unsatisfied longing. My body was screaming at me to orgasm, *oh God, why can't he just make me orgasm like before?*

"I thought you would be tired, but I couldn't wait to show you. Would you rather rest first? Or—"

"No," I said in a rush. "No. I want to paint."

"Paint, then," he said. "I want to see what you're feeling right now. Paint what is going on in that innocent mind." He smirked.

"Right," I said. He was well aware what was going on in my mind, and none of it was innocent.

I walked over and examined the canvases. God, these weren't the cheap ones I always worked with. The frames were solid and the canvas was a quality linen that had already been prepared for painting.

I went back to the table and opened the cabinets. I tried not to gasp my surprise at the assortment of paints in front of me. Spray paint, oils, acrylics by the gallon. There were delicate brushes of a few hairs, and thick brushes, wedge-shaped, bleached at the ends. There were rollers of different textures, layering palette knives of all different shapes and sizes. There was everything I needed and more.

"I can use any of this stuff?" I asked. My fingers reached out, touching the materials in wonder.

"Any of it. Except for the storage area, which is locked." He pointed to the black door that had a padlock on the outside hinge. "That's not to be touched. Understood?"

"Understood," I said, still gaping at the paints. Lord, this was thousands of dollars' worth of paint sitting on this table. Maybe tens of thousands. And not the cheapo stuff, either.

He smiled a bit at my expression before turning away to leave.

"Where are you going?" I asked, before he had taken two steps. There was amusement in his eyes as he looked back at me.

"I'm going to get us breakfast. You will stay in here and paint."

"And if I don't?" It wasn't a real question. I just wanted to see the spark light up his eyes again.

"If you don't obey me, you'll be punished. The same goes for if you touch yourself. Understood?"

I flushed. Even with all that he had done to me, touching myself in front of him made me turn red with imagined embarrassment.

"Understood." It was a squeak coming from my mouth. I didn't know why he had chosen me. I wasn't special. I wasn't nearly as beautiful as the girls who had swarmed his party.

All of those thoughts dropped away, though, when I looked back at the blank canvases waiting for me to put my mark on them.

Maybe that's what he saw in me. That, and... loneliness.

I didn't think a billionaire could know what it was like to be lonely, but maybe...

Jake cleared his throat. He pushed himself away from the doorframe and turned to go.

"I'll be back shortly," he said. "Enjoy."

***

I painted.

It had been a while since I'd painted on an actual canvas, and in good light. All of my street art had been thrown up hastily, in dark alleyways or on subway cars in the train yard at night. I never got a good look at what I was painting, not really.

110

The first canvas I picked up was one of the bigger ones. Without too much preamble, I tossed it down onto the floor and headed back for the cabinets to pick out the paint.

Back when I was in elementary school, part of the ritual I had for painting was arranging all of my paints and brushes beforehand, getting everything ready before I started. I'd set my brushes out carefully, lining them up next to the paper. Slowly, meticulously.

Since living in New York City, I'd learned how to work as a street artist. I never got a chance to settle in before painting—I simply didn't have the time. Security guards would be patrolling, and I had to paint out of my backpack with cans and brushes that I threw haphazardly back to make a run for it if I saw anyone coming.

So if you'd told me that I had a room full of painting supplies all to myself, I would have told you that I would take my time. I would go slow. I would savor the moment.

But I didn't.

I don't know what it was. The sleepless night, maybe, or the drugs they'd used to knock me out. Mostly, though, I thought it was the face that Jake Carville had spent the past hour teasing me past the point of sanity, and I didn't have any mental energy left to think about the painting I was going to do.

So I just painted.

I didn't bother to take out all of the paints and lay them out, or pick out all of the brushes I would use. I went for it, grabbing a handful of brushes and an armful of paint tubes. Without forethought, I squeezed the paint onto one of the plastic mixing palettes and started. No ceremony, no ritual. Nothing but pure emotion.

First, green. Green like his eyes. That would be the background. I smeared the brush back and forth, adding daubs of black when I needed to make the color richer, the values more contrasting.

As I painted, I remembered what he'd done to me. My frustrations surged through me and erupted out onto the canvas. The strokes of his fingers became strokes of my paintbrush.

I painted quickly, the way I wanted him to touch me. The brush roughed across the canvas in thick sheets. There was nothing in me to tell me to stop, that I was using too much paint. There was no restraint to tell me I should go slower. There was nothing but the furious insistent beat of my heart as I worked the canvas to its natural end.

I used a small brush to pick up beads of gold paint, spattering them over the deep emerald color with abandon. I didn't wait for it to dry.

Then I painted a swath of rich dark red diagonally. A stripe of darkness, like a blindfold over the eyes. Looking at it, I could see all of my frustration on the stretched fabric. I could see the strokes of the brush hairs.

Standing up from the canvas, I felt dizzy. Had it been a minute or an hour? Paint spattered my ankles, and I'd gotten smears of green and gold on the bottom of the white terrycloth robe. I looked around. He wasn't back yet.

I'd finished a canvas. Did he mean for me to paint more?

There were so many canvases here. So many blank spaces. The white of the room and the increasing brightness of the rising sun turned the white squares and rectangles brilliant with light. Brilliant and yet empty, with nothing painted on them. All around me was pure, pure white.

Something inside me broke. The neediness in my body was converted to a manic whirlwind of painting. Stepping to one wall, I picked up a large canvas, threw it down onto the ground at that spot, and began to paint furiously.

Jake had held back so much. He had given me a taste of what he could deliver, and then he had pulled it back. For the whole night he had teased me, hanging satisfaction just out of my reach. Dangling my desires in front of me, then pulling them away.

Now he had given me this, and I would take it. I wouldn't wait for him. I wouldn't be ashamed. I would take it, all of it.

I painted another canvas, then another. Paint smeared all over my hands and ankles. I used the white robe as a towel to clean off my hands when I needed to. I used the edge of the robe to swipe at misplaced brushstrokes. The terrycloth robe grew heavier as paint soaked into its edges, until I looked like I should be heading over to Broadway to star in a production of *Joseph and the Technicolor Dreamcoat.*

I filled my canvases with my longing. Flowers grew, straggling across the white, bleeding violet and goldenrod where their leaves stretched forward. I painted all of the images that I dreamed of painting, painted and painted and it still wasn't enough.

At my feet were half a dozen paintings, rough, frenzied works. None of them were what I needed. I looked wildly at the other walls to find a space that would fit the sweeping colors that whirled in my head.

Blank canvases all around, none what I had in mind. The flowers didn't work, fitted in the square of a single space. I didn't know what I needed. Something bigger, maybe.

I looked only once at the door to the storage area, wondering if there were other canvases inside. But no. He'd been very serious about staying away from there.

Break in and maybe he'll punish you again.

I scolded my mind for the thought. A faint heat rose to my skin, even as I tried to quash it.

Then I saw it.

It wasn't a canvas at all. It was a space on the wall in the corner of the room. The light from a skylight fell perfectly into the corner, radiating brightness all around.

That was what I needed.

I picked up the bucket of green paint and headed there.

I mixed black in with the green on the wall. And impulsively, I grabbed a spray paint can.

Lace.

It was my name. It was my tag.

The green went on in wide strokes, and I'd barely finished the contours of the letters before coming back with the can of black. My arm swung wide, not outlining the letters but instead marking the shadows that the letters would cast if they were there.

I was normally quite precise, but my emotions were running so high that my finger slipped once, and once only. The extra blast of paint dripped, dripped. It would ruin the effect.

Unthinking, I undid the tie from the bathrobe and slipped the tie off. I used it to press against the wall, mopping up the stray drip. A glimmer of white from behind the paint showed through. Yes. That was what it needed. I scraped away paint in soft curves, highlighting the swells of the letters where the light shone.

I stepped back and admired it. It was possibly the best version that I'd ever done. The effect was three-dimensional, the shadows and highlights making the tag stand out.

I was finished. My breaths came hard, and I wiped the beads of sweat off of my brow. I'd done it. It was perfect. I stared at it, willing it to seep into my brain so I could recreate it on another wall, somewhere that wasn't in a billionaire's apartment.

Oh, crap.

This was his apartment.

He'd told me to paint, but he surely didn't mean that I could paint the walls. It was a horrible mistake to do this. What… what was I thinking?

You weren't thinking. You were feeling.

Behind me, I heard the door open again. I whirled around to see Jake standing in the doorway, a silver tray in his hands.

115

He took me in. Standing there in an untied robe coated with paint, my bra and panties exposed. Paint spattered all over my limbs. And on the corner wall of his perfect apartment, my tag. His eyes widened.

"I'm sorry," I whispered.

Chapter Four

I stared at Jake, my heart sinking. I'd defaced his walls. Blood rushed to my face.

He set the silver tray down. I noticed with the part of my mind that was numb that there were two cups of something hot; the steam rose as he put the tray on the floor. He stood up and crossed the room quickly, his strides long and determined.

I was stammering out another apology when he reached me.

He pushed me back against the wall. Kissed my neck. I barely had time to breathe before his hands moved down, yanking the robe from my shoulders.

"Oh!" I cried. "You're getting paint on your—ah!"

He bit at my neck, a bite on the shoulder as though he was claiming me. He buried his face in my hair, his hands pinning my arms back. The paint was still wet behind me, and cold for only a second before he licked my neck and flames took my body whole.

My hands moved down to his chest, tentatively at first. I had paint all over me, and every touch smeared red and green and blue onto his suit. But it was ruined already, and when his hands found my ass I couldn't care at all about it.

Kisses, kisses everywhere but my face. His hands gripped my ass and squeezed and I cried aloud.

He picked me up and shoved me against the wall. I wrapped my legs around his waist and he buried his head in the crook of my neck, pressing kisses all the way down from my ear to my collarbone.

I tried desperately to shift his mouth up to mine, but he would not kiss me directly. My lips burned.

"Kiss me," I whispered. I wasn't sure if I was allowed to speak during sex, but I wanted this so badly.

He pulled back and looked at me.

"Not yet, Lacey," he said. There was a threat in his face that told me to take him seriously. I couldn't help feeling a pang of rejection, but when his hands moved down over my body the pang turned to a violent shock of desire.

We were pressed against my paint, my *art*, but I didn't care one bit if I was messing it up. I felt the paint smear over my back as he slid down slowly, easing me down by inches.

His ruined jacket flew back over his shoulder. He unbuttoned his shirt. One sleeve at a time, the clothes peeled away. He left on his white undershirt. I could see the fabric straining against the muscles of his arms.

Then I realized what he was doing.

He buried his face in between my legs. His hands gripped my thighs tightly and his teeth pulled my panties down. I was wet and the chill of the air was nothing compared to the burning desire that shot through my every nerve.

He licked me and I came instantly.

Bucking against his hard hands, the orgasm raced through me in thick waves of pleasure.

"Ohh!" I cried out, shaking so hard my head knocked against the wall. *"Oh God, yes! YES!"*

I shuddered again and again against his hot tongue that was still licking, pressing against me. He kissed my swollen sex and I jerked again as the last thrill of the orgasm rode through me. This—was this what sex was truly like? None of my masturbation sessions could hold a candle to the raging orgasms that Jake was able to tear from me so easily.

It had ripped through my body so quickly that I hadn't even found the time to be embarrassed. My whole body shivered like it was made of liquid held together by the barest film. My chest heaved with breaths as I tried to gain enough air to stand on my own. Right now I was leaning against the wall and he was holding me up.

I blinked hard and looked down. He was still kneeling between my legs, and now shame came tumbling in.

How... why...? I had no answers. I didn't even have the questions. I only knew that this wasn't a fair game, that somehow he had gotten the upper hand again even as he knelt and pressed his cheek against my thigh.

He heard my breathing slow and turned his face up. He was smiling.

"Again," he whispered.

It wasn't a question, and although I struggled to break from his grip, my efforts were half-hearted. The orgasm was still shivering my body with its force as he whispered the word against my overly sensitive clit. His breath was warm and oh so tempting.

I put my hands down on his shoulders, meaning to press him away. The paint on my back was sticky; drops ran down the backs of my arms. He was spotted with paint, too, and the more I looked at him the more I noticed that my work had gotten all over him.

"Your suit," I said in weak protest.

"It's already done for," he said, and he sounded as if he didn't mind a bit. A bespoke suit, it probably had cost him thousands and thousands of dollars. And he tossed the jacket aside and smeared paint over the pants... for what?

For me.

Heat streaked down my legs as he pressed an open kiss against me down there. He hadn't kissed me yet on the mouth and I wanted so badly to know what he tasted like.

Later, he'd said. Later? When I'd first met him, at the party, he said that I was to be his gift for a week. I wondered if he would get bored with me before then.

I wondered if it would be enough time.

A pinch on my asscheek made me squeal. His grinning face told me that he wasn't about to let my thoughts go wandering off again. A swipe of his tongue brought forth another squeal. I never knew that I could sound so girly.

"You know, I'm not a very patient man," Jake said. His tongue moved again, hot against my folds. Exploring... probing...

I moaned when he pulled back slightly. He pressed a kiss to the inside of my thigh, although it was slick with moisture. It tickled slightly and I jerked back, but his hands gripped me in a solid vise.

"I love the noises you make, sweet girl," he said. He sucked at me then, and explosions of color burst behind my eyelids. I didn't even know that I had closed my eyes. Immediately I thought of the canvases, of the painted wall behind me. That was how I had painted my frustration.

How would I paint this? This fury of burning pressure that had already rekindled in my body? How else but red, red and orange and gold, the color of flame? Or blue, flame's true color, the hottest part of the spectrum. All of the colors, in fact, all except green, his eyes.

Before I met him, I never thought that green could smolder.

His hands kneaded the backs of my asscheeks, pulling my hips forward. I screamed softly as his tongue thrust into me, then retreated, then thrust again. My hands had moved down to push him away, but now my fingers threaded his hair and pulled him urgently to me.

"Yes," I whispered. I tilted my head back. The ceiling, too, was white, pure white, and just above me the green dripped like a dark growth. The paint was all over, in my hair and on my body, and I didn't care a single bit. All I cared about was the insistent rhythm with which he thrust his tongue farther, farther inside of me.

The slickness, the press of his lips, the suction that ebbed and grew, all tore me from side to side. The room had turned hot again and I was breathing hard, my throat burning along with the rest of me.

Clenching my eyes shut, embarrassment forgotten, I screamed loud as the pressure exploded again through me, bursting like color from a brush onto a perfectly white canvas. I threw my head from side to side, clawing at his back, his hair. His tongue worked me all through the orgasm, pushing me to ever greater heights and sending me flying from the top.

Every muscle in my body had turned watery and I trembled as he leaned back, wiping his mouth on his undershirt. I nearly sobbed with pleasure. Every new climax he brought me to was higher than the last, and I could not understand how. How had he pulled these sensations from my body?

This is what I want to paint. This.

I thought it dizzily, not sure what I meant. My hands were still opening and closing against the hair on his head.

He stood up, his hands pressing first against my hips, then cupping my elbows. I stayed leaning against the wall, breathless and unable to stand. My eyes closed, I felt his lips brush the top of my hairline.

"When do you want me to fuck you?" he whispered.

The question shocked me. It was meant to shock me. I opened my eyes, swallowing. Jake grinned wolfishly.

I gathered myself for a moment. He was pushing me to the edge again, this time to the edge of my discomfort. He must know how difficult it was for me to talk. Not just because he'd taken away my breath, but because… well, I had never talked about sex before with a guy.

"I don't know."

"What do you mean, you don't know?"

I shook my head, feeling my brain slosh around in a pleasant haze.

"I don't know," I said again.

"Come on. How innocent are you, my Lacey?"

My Lacey. Was I his? Yes. Yes, he'd bought me. He hadn't bought me with money, though. He bought me with his touches, strokes that sent my body whirling in a storm of pleasure and needing more. More.

He thought of me as a girl, and now he was asking me to tell him. There was no thought in my mind that I wouldn't tell him. He would know soon enough. I'd heard about the blood, and the pain, not too bad, they said.

I couldn't lie to him. I steadied myself as best as I could and then lifted my head, speaking as clearly, as matter-of-factly as I could.

"I'm a virgin."

***

Jake's eyes stormed over, and for the first time since I'd met him, his emotions showed bare and obvious on his face. One in particular.

I could see in his eyes a small flicker of fear.

"A virgin?" he asked.

His skin was taut over his forehead. Sweat darkened his white undershirt, showing the damp skin through the fabric. He looked like a wild animal coiled and ready to attack. I let myself breathe in slowly before replying.

"Yes."

"How old are you?"

The last thrills of the orgasm were leaving me under his eyes. He looked so fierce. Almost angry. I frowned back at him, crossing my arms over my chest.

"Did you even bother looking up my name?"

"I've only had a few hours, and most of your records are sealed. All of them, in fact. But you knew that, of course."

Yes. My parents had paid money to scrub away my teenage crimes. They'd been ashamed, and now as I thought about it, the disappointment they'd shown made me feel utterly guilty.

They'd punished me back then, too, of course. Not physically, they weren't that kind of people. I'd hated the punishment. But their shame made me feel so wrong that it hurt me all over again.

I shook my head. Why did my mind fly to all of my bad memories when I thought back to that time?

"An article on your high school website showed you graduated five years ago, with your name in the list of graduates. I assumed—"

"I got my GED at the end of middle school and went to work on my parents' farm," I said, thinking about the two-story white building sitting in the middle of a cluster of low oaks.

"Middle school?"

"Yes."

He sat down, his face pale. He was sitting in a puddle of paint that I'd dropped earlier, the dark indigo now seeping into the gray of his pants. It looked like a bloodstain on the side of his leg, as if he'd been shot.

When he spoke again, he spoke in one sharp breath, as though he'd gotten the wind knocked out of him.

"How old are you, Lacey?"

I knelt beside him. His eyes searched mine for the answer. I couldn't hold out any longer. It was torture to him, I could see that.

And, unlike him, I could not stand to torture.

"Twenty-one."

He exhaled. Relief rippled through his muscled arms and he swallowed. His chest bellowed out against his white undershirt smeared with a rainbow of paint.

He rubbed his temples with his fingertips, sliding them to the bridge of his nose and then back.

"I'm sorry. You don't know— you can't know."

Know what? I kept myself from speaking the words. He would give me his past when he wanted to. I could sense that pressing him would make him recoil from me.

"How old are you?" I asked.

He smiled.

"Thirty-one."

"That's not that old."

"There's a world of difference. Once you're out of college—"

"I'm not in college. I never went to college."

He looked at me anew.

"Of course. That's right."

"Stop looking at me like you just figured something out about me," I said.

"Is that how I'm looking at you?"

"Don't talk down to me." Irritation surged through my chest. "You don't know anything about me. I'm not some pampered rich kid like you, okay? I had to grow up early."

"I'm sorry. You're right."

He patted the ground next to him. I sat, careful to avoid the indigo puddle even though I was covered in paint. My back itched from where the paint was drying. When he looked at me, his eyes searched mine.

"Tell me about yourself, Lacey."

Chapter Five

The sun had almost reached the top of the Manhattan skyrise buildings. We sat in the middle of the room full of canvases and talked as the room warmed with its light.

We ate from the silver tray he'd brought. There was a full tea set with cream and sugar. A heap of pancakes was topped with strawberries and handwhipped cream, and another plate was laden high with bacon and eggs.

I reached for the pancakes and he stopped my hand with a touch of his wrist.

"Let me feed you," he said.

I was uncertain, but I bit my lip. He was trying to do something for me, I realized. Something nice. Something… innocent.

"Strawberry, please," I said.

He picked up a strawberry from the side of the dish and dragged it through the whipped cream. He lifted it to my lips.

It was the sweetest strawberry I'd ever tasted. I licked my lips and saw him look away. Good. Maybe he would feel some of the unsatisfied desire that I'd felt before.

"These remind me of the strawberries we had on the farm," I said. "They were smaller, but just as delicious."

"You worked on a farm? Really?"

"Yeah."

"What does that mean?"

"What do you think it means?"

"Living on a farm? I don't know. I've never been to a farm," he said.

I grinned. It was nice to feel like I had some experiences that he hadn't had already. Lord knows he was way ahead of me when it came to sex. But at least I was ahead of him when it came to farming.

"We did some homesteading, so there was always harvesting or weeding or canning to do. Mornings you feed the chickens, evenings you go gather eggs. You know, farming stuff."

"That's fascinating." He leaned forward, his hand stroking one side of his cheek. Wow. He really was fascinated by nothing.

"I had a vanilla bean plant," I said.

"What does a vanilla bean plant look like?"

"It's a vine. Grew it right up a string in the greenhouse. I thought it would taste like vanilla ice cream. When a bean finally got ripe, I bit into it."

"Isn't real vanilla—"

"It's the worst!" I grimaced while remembering it. "So bitter it stung my tongue. My dad laughed and laughed."

"What is your family like?"

"They're fine. Nice. Normal. My mom makes the best quilts and my dad yells at the TV during political debates and baseball."

I cupped my chin in my hand.

"How about you?" I asked.

"Me?" He looked surprised for a moment, then relaxed. "Oh, that's right. I forget that you don't know anything about me."

"The elusive Jake Carville."

For a second, his mouth turned down at both corners. Then he composed his face into a teasing expression.

"Am I that elusive? I'm all over TV, you know."

I shrugged.

"I don't have a TV. So sue me."

"I think I'm beginning to realize why…"

"Why what?"

"Nothing. Nothing," he said. "So why are you here?"

"Here? I'm here because an eccentric oversexed billionaire kidnapped me and brought me here."

That brought a smile to Jake's face. A real smile, one that crinkled the corners of his eyes. It made him look even more handsome, if that was possible. He forked a piece of pancake up and held it out to me. I took the bite gratefully.

"No, I mean, why are you here in New York City?"

I sighed. I remembered the farm, remembered leaving it, waving goodbye to my mom. My dad had already gone out to the fields to finish the harvest. He wasn't ever much for goodbyes. Even when I called them, he would grunt a few hellos over the phone and then pass it on to the rest of the family.

Why was I here? I had almost forgotten over the past year.

"I moved here when I realized that Iowa wasn't exactly the place to make it as a budding artist."

"So you're here as an artist."

"Sort of. I mean, I'm trying. I saved up enough money for a train ticket and a small room to sublet, and I came out here. Now I'm waitressing and bartending. Doing absolutely everything except art. Well, I do art when I can."

I thought of the subway cars, of spray paint cans and paint markers. Of running away from security guards who caught me painting flowers on the aluminum siding.

I yawned, cupping a hand to my mouth.

"You must be so tired."

"A little." The pancakes had settled into the bottom of my stomach, and my stupidly high libido had calmed down. The previous night was starting to catch up with me. When had I slept last? I didn't even remember.

"Let's get you to bed."

"Okay. Wait! I have to call in sick for work." My boss at the diner would kill me if I didn't show up. I was supposed to be there at eleven, and I was pretty sure I wasn't going to make it in at all. Oh well. I'd never taken a sick day before. She could deal with it.

"I'll take care of it."

"Okay."

He sounded so gentle, so sure. He would take care of everything. Of course. He had control, didn't he? Complete control.

***

He picked me up in both arms, as before. But this time, he held me so gently that I could have sworn I was floating on clouds. My head lolled against his shoulder. All of the paint on me had dried over my skin and underwear.

I was tired, so tired. If I had a few cups of coffee, I would have been okay to work. In my mind, I could see all of the disgruntled customers. The endless plates of food. My boss, pacing the floor.

But it was okay to take a sick day. That would be fine. He would call. Jake would call them. And I would sleep...

Where would I sleep?

I lifted my head from his shoulder and peered ahead. He was carrying me down the hallway. I could see the paintings on either side of me, their elaborately carved wood frames glinting and gilded. The carpet, plush like the thick grass that used to grow under the oak tree in my backyard.

"Where are we going?" I mumbled.

"So curious. We're taking you to bed."

"To your bed?"

The expression on his face showed a slight shock, and his next step was quicker. He strode down the hallway to another door, this one diagonal to the art studio.

"No. No, of course not."

"Jake?"

Again the slight wince, and I felt guilty. I'd forgotten that he didn't like me to use his name.

"I'm sorry," I said quickly. A flush spread over my cheeks. How could I ask him anything so intimate? But I had to know.

131

"Are you going to sleep with me?"

He opened the door with a blank face. I couldn't read his eyes. Did he still want me? I needed to know.

"Please—"

"Not right now, Lacey. Now, I need you to go to sleep."

Sleep. As soon as he said the word, it was like a command. A yawn rose from my chest, and my eyes watered sleepily. I rubbed one eye with the back of my hand.

He set me down in the bed, and the covers were on top of me before I could even reach for them. He tucked the blanket in around my shoulders. God, it was soft. And warm. So warm...

"Sleep," he said. And then, the last thing I heard from him before I passed out completely. "You'll need your rest."

***

I woke up before he came into the room. The blankets around me were so soft. The room was dim, the only light was a thin stream of lamplight from the hallway.

Beautiful, I thought in a daze. The painting in this room across from my bed was lit slightly by the hallway light. It was a pastoral scene, one of the old masters. Lambs on a hillside. They reminded me of the farm back in Iowa.

A hand pushed the door open and I blinked again sleepily. It was Jake in the doorway. Jake, who'd fed me pancakes this morning. I smiled.

He was holding something, and as he came closer to the bed I saw what it was. A dress, a long evening dress. It was blue and silken, flowing over his arms like a waterfall.

"Waterfalls are white," I mumbled. That was something I'd learned while painting. Water isn't blue, really. It's every color of the rainbow. All it does is reflect the world around it.

"Are you awake?" Jake asked. He sat down next to me on the bed and lay the dress on the foot of it.

Ha. A dress. He'd brought me a dress. But of course, he couldn't know that I didn't wear dresses. I never wore dresses.

"I wanted to take you out to dinner," he was saying.

"Dinner?" I blinked. His eyes shone green even in the dim light. I blinked again.

"Yes."

All of my senses came back to me in a sharp flash. I sat up in bed, my hands still clutching the covers.

"What—what time is it?" I asked. My mouth felt like cotton.

"It's seven o'clock."

"At night?"

Jake raised his eyebrows, and I yanked the covers off of me, not caring if he saw my robe open up. Then I remembered. He was supposed to call.

"Did you call them?" I asked, panic still choking my throat.

"Call who?"

"My work. To say I wasn't coming in."

133

"Oh, right. No. I'll call them now if you like."

"What?!"

Oh my God. My boss would be furious at me. Not Casper, although I'm pretty sure he'd be wondering why I had left the back door open and taken off without saying goodbye. But my boss at the diner… she was much, much less nice.

My mom told me not to say anything bad about anyone else if I could help it. *If you don't have something nice to say, don't say anything at all.*

So I never talked about my boss much.

I was pretty sure, though, that the man standing in front of me with a sexy smile had just cost me my job. And, mean boss or not, it was the best job I had.

"How *could* you?"

"What?" Jake frowned slightly, cocking his head. I tugged on the covers, but he was sitting on them. I couldn't get out of the bed.

"You let me oversleep and you didn't even call up my work to say that I was sick!"

"I thought you needed your sleep."

Argh! He sounded so… so reasonable! Like I was the one who was crazy!

"I need a job more than I need my sleep," I said, explaining it to him slowly.

"For what?"

For what. He really said that.

"For what? For money. Hello?"

"I already wrote you a check for your rent," he said, tilting his head. I tugged again at the covers but they held tight. I blew air between my teeth.

"That's not... *I have to have a job!*"

"Why?"

"Well for one, that money won't last forever. And what will I do when it runs out?"

"I can write you another check," he said, squinting at me like I was an alien species. God, he was so handsome. A stirring inside of my body made me even angrier at myself. And at him. Mostly at him.

"That's not what I want!" I cried.

"What do you want?"

I plopped back down on the bed, my mouth loosely parted. The pillows billowed around my head.

"I don't understand you at all," I said.

"What do you want? You don't want to work as a waitress forever, do you?"

"Well, no, but—" I stammered.

"Then think of this as a gift to help you along to something you actually want to do. You want to make art. Whatever you need to pay your bills, you can have. It's fine."

"I can't just take your money," I said. I felt like I was speaking another language to him. Like we were tribes from opposite sides of the world, and money had a different meaning.

"The money doesn't make any difference to me," he said gently. "And it obviously makes a difference to you. So take it and use it."

I slumped back against the pillows, looking toward the ceiling. I breathed in and out. It was weird. I actually felt *rested*. I didn't remember ever feeling like I'd gotten enough sleep before.

"This is ridiculous," I said.

"You're ridiculous for being so stubborn. Will you take the money?"

I looked at him and opened my mouth, then closed it. Then opened it again. Then closed it again. He obviously wasn't going to give in, and I obviously wasn't going to get out of this bed without him letting me take his money. I sighed.

"Yes. Fine. Thank you," I said. "I... I don't mean to sound ungrateful. I just don't... I've never been offered anything like this before."

I swallowed hard, clutching the covers under my fingers.

"You're welcome," he said gently.

"So. Uh. Dinner?" I asked, echoing his words from before.

"If you would like. Lacey, I didn't realize... you're younger than I expected. I'll understand if you want to take the check and leave."

I shook my head, my cheeks flushing. I'd been called young my whole life. I'd gotten a fake ID when I was thirteen so that I could work with my brothers at the neighboring farms. Everyone knew, but the money was under the table and it was an excuse for the people who were hiring me.

When I moved to New York City, the fake ID came in very handy. I didn't try to get into bars with it, but bar work—that was a different story. At twenty-one, I'd done more bartending jobs that most thirty year old bartenders I knew.

"If it's about the money… if you need more, I can give you more. It's no problem."

I should have taken it. Just grabbed the check and ran. It was a year's rent, and I could scrounge up another job without too much trouble. Even in this economy, a young girl could make her way as a bartender in NYC.

But I didn't want to go. I was curious. I—I wanted to have dinner with him.

"I'll stay," I said, shrugging in what I hoped was a casual manner. "I came back here, didn't I?"

"Are you sure? I won't ask you again, Lacey. You've already gotten two second chances with me. Most don't receive that luxury."

I saw his throat muscles tighten. Another glimmer in his eye. God, he was attractive. I didn't care if he was more than ten years older than me. He looked like he had more than taken care of himself over those ten years. His muscles were broad, his chin dark with stubble. His mouth—

I tore my eyes away from his beautiful face.

"Yes," I said, staring down at his belt. Leather, with a silver buckle that reflected the decor of the room. As he stood up, I watched the reflection shift, twisting me along with the rest of the bed inside of it.

His hand reached out. Mindlessly, I took it. He pulled me up from the bed and I stood in front of him.

"God. Lacey, you're beautiful," he said breathlessly. His eyes were palpable as they moved down over my skin.

My paint-spattered skin.

"I have to wash up before I get dressed for dinner," I said.

"I know. The bathroom is just this way." He gestured, tugging my hand so that I would walk over with him.

"I can figure out how to work a shower," I said, a bit irritated. I was young, but I wasn't a child.

"I know you can. But this week, you're mine, and you will follow my orders." His hand clamped down on my wrist and I followed him.

Mine. The word coming out of his mouth sounded like a cage around me. A gilded cage, shiny and new, decorated with the most beautiful ornaments.

A cage I wanted to be in.

Chapter Six

Jake let my wrist go and stepped forward into the bathroom.

The room itself was all white marble, but the tub looked as though it had been carved out of a huge slab of volcanic rock—it was black, and as he turned the faucets on, white steam rose from the splashing water.

He adjusted the temperature of the water, then turned around, still sitting on the edge of the tub.

"Take off that robe," he said.

I flushed. He had already seen my naked breasts—heck, he'd put my shirt on last night after I passed out, hadn't he? Still, it felt strange to undress in front of a man. It was something I'd never done before.

I tugged the robe off of my shoulders. He drew a sharp breath as he looked over my body. I tossed the robe onto the ground.

"Now your panties," he said.

God, his voice was something else. When he told me to do something, it wasn't even a thought in my mind to disobey. It was like he was controlling my movements. More than that, the low growl of his words sent shivers through me.

My eyelashes fluttered as I shimmied my panties down to my ankles and then stepped out of them completely. I took two steps to the bath, wanting to get in the tub and out of his eyes.

He caught me by the wrist before I could step in.

"Wait just one moment," he said.

I felt awful. In the bright light, he could see all my lumps and creases, all of the parts of me that bulged out where they shouldn't. But in his eyes, I didn't see the disgust that I feared.

Instead, I saw nothing but desire.

His tongue dipped out against his bottom lip. Goosebumps rose on my arms, not because of the chill. The way he was looking at me—I wanted him to look at me that way forever. I would do anything for him.

"Alright," he said finally. "Get in."

The water steamed around my legs as I stepped up and into the bath. I lay back against the obsidian edge of the tub. It was rounded. I sighed as the heat seeped into my pores, warming me through and through.

"Give me your foot," he said.

My jaw dropped.

"What—"

"No questions," he scolded gently. "Give me your foot."

I raised my leg and he took my foot in his hand. He reached for the washcloth on the side of the tub and began to wash me. The white washcloth scrubbed the acrylic paints easily off of my skin.

It was strange to feel him rubbing between my toes. The feeling was oddly sensual. He massaged the soles of my feet and I couldn't help letting out a soft moan of pleasure.

"I'm glad you like this," he said.

A foot massage in a steaming bath with a sexy millionaire washing me? What's not to like? But I didn't say anything. I just let him wash me, the washcloth moving across my skin. He moved up to my legs and washed me there, the paint flaking away and settling to the bottom of the tub.

"It's a shame," I said idly.

"A shame?"

"To wash off all the paint. It was nice while it lasted."

Jake smiled at me. He motioned for my other foot. I bit my lip as I lifted it up for him to wash. As his hands moved up along my ankles, my calves, I held my breath and wondered what he would do once he moved up all the way between my thighs. The thought sent burning pangs of arousal through me.

"Where do you paint? Here in the city? A gallery?"

He had me. I stared down at the water, flicking the surface lightly with my fingertips.

"I paint… I paint everywhere."

"Everywhere?" He raised an eyebrow.

"Yes, graffiti, if that's what you're asking. I don't have a lot of other options."

"You use your real name, though. Lace…"

"Yeah. I like my name. Although it got me in big trouble when I was a kid."

"Tell me."

I looked up at him. Rather than being judgmental, he seemed intrigued by my admission. I took a breath, inhaling the sweet scent of soap.

"One time I got this painting in my head. It always starts with a blank space, you know? There was this blank space on the back of one of the corn silos we shared with the neighbors. And I thought it would be the perfect place for one of my flowers."

"You paint flowers?"

"Silly, right? Like, I'm not a girly girl at all. But I've always loved painting flowers. Something about the way the light goes right through the petals. It's like they're shining from the inside."

"That sounds wonderful," he murmured.

"Oh, you have paint under your fingernails too. Right there." I pointed to his hands which were rubbing my knee gently. There were specks of lavender under his nails at his fingertips.

"Must have gotten them dirty last night," he said absently. He scrubbed the paint off.

I frowned. I hadn't used lavender paint on any of the canvases, I didn't think. Not the spray kind that was under his nails. But then he was rinsing his hands and I forgot all about it.

He moved back to my body, the washcloth forgotten. His hands slipped between my thighs before I could say another word. I gasped, jerking back in the water, but there was nowhere to go. His green eyes bored into me as I gripped his arm, startled.

"Lacey," he said. "You promised to obey me when you decided to stay here. Do you remember?"

My heart thudded against my chest. Steam rose up and fogged the air in the bathroom, giving everything a hazy, dreamlike quality.

"Yes," I whispered. The word soaked into the air and was lost. I could feel the tips of his fingers pressing lightly against my inner thigh underneath the water. The sensation was delicate, but the effects of his touch were not. Heat swirled through my core, aching to be released.

"Good," he said. "Now relax and let me wash you."

***

"Lean your head back," he ordered.

There was a curved spot in the obsidian rock of the tub. I rested my head there. His fingers—oh God, his fingers were there, right there between my legs. I could feel his hand grazing my skin, sending lightning bolts of desire through every nerve ending.

"Close your eyes."

I obeyed, but I shifted uncomfortably in the water.

"Why do you want my eyes closed?" I asked.

"It stretches your other senses," Jake said. His hand moved back down to my knee, then up the other leg, only lightly touching my thigh. I shivered in the warm water, feeling myself clench involuntarily down there. He continued speaking, and now that my eyes were closed I could hear every nuance, every low rumble in his voice.

"As an artist, you spend all of your hours looking at things, seeing the lines and spaces of the world. Sometimes you have to slow down and take in the other senses."

"How do you know? Are you an artist?"

"Of sorts."

143

His hand moved up, up, then grazed my aching slit. I moaned in the sweet darkness as his fingertips slid over my wet and swollen sex, teasing me. My back arched, needing his fingers in me. Needing more.

He pulled away, and I whimpered.

"Now, then," he said. "I told you to relax and I mean it."

Relax? How could he expect me to relax when his every touch had me jumping out of my skin. But I did my best. *Breathe in. Breathe out.*

The washcloth came back and pressed against my stomach, rubbing gently. He didn't miss a single square inch as he worked his way up my chest. He paused at my breasts, cupping one in his bare hands. I gasped as the washcloth rubbed over my nipple, making it harden and ache.

His mouth on my nipple, sucking. His tongue—

Oh, God, I didn't know if I could keep my eyes closed. My imagination was too strong, and the images going through my head right now couldn't be chased away by mere willpower. With every touch he sent ripples of pleasure through my body.

He massaged my arms, my hands. His fingers intertwined with mine, the soapy grip making me mad with lustful thoughts. I imagined his hands all over me. His fingers, the way he'd thrust them into me last night, the way he'd sent me into a shivering liquid orgasm…

As though reading my thoughts, he chuckled and rubbed my hands once more, leaving them to float helplessly in the water. He came around the back of the tub, rubbing my shoulders. I groaned as he worked my muscles, kneading them until I was a tub of goo. I couldn't have opened my eyes if I tried, that's how relaxed I felt.

His hands moved up to my head, and I felt his fingers begin to work their way through my hair, rubbing circles against my scalp. I breathed in and smelled the scent of the shampoo he was using.

"Mmm, lavender," I said. The shampoo had such a delicate scent of lavender, with faint touches of honey. It was almost like being back on the farm, in the late afternoon, when the smells of the flowers rose from the fields.

His hands were strong, cupping the back of my head. I let myself rest in his palms as he rinsed out the shampoo and worked conditioner in through my hair. God, his fingertips were phenomenal. I wanted to suck on them.

Where did I get these thoughts? I hadn't ever had sex, hadn't gone farther than kissing a guy, but when Jake touched me it was as though every dirty daydream I had leapt to life inside of me. I ached between my thighs. Would he come back down and satisfy me, the way he had before?

I waited and waited, my arousal heightened with every touch of his hands. He rinsed my hair, then rinsed my body.

"You can open your eyes," he said.

I did. The room seemed unnaturally bright, white with steam. He wasn't touching me, though. He was patting his hands dry on a towel.

I whimpered. He had gotten me all aroused and didn't let me come.

"Will you…" I trailed the end of the sentence off. He looked at me, naked in the tub, and I could see the glint of amusement in his eyes as he shook his head. I reached to touch myself. I needed relief.

"Then let me—"

"Don't."

His voice caught me by surprise, seizing my hand before I could touch between my legs.

"Why not?" I asked, hating the whine in my voice.

"You have a lot of questions for someone who's supposed to be obeying orders."

"You never ordered me not to ask questions," I countered.

He laughed slightly.

"True," he said, holding out the towel. "Don't come yet. I will let you know when. Tonight I want you ready for me."

I'm always ready for you.

I shook the dirty thought out of my head. Here I was, never having slept with a man before, wanting to tell him that he could have me whenever he wanted.

He could, though. I knew from the way his hands slipped over my body that I would be ready for him when he wanted me. I was ready now, now and always.

"Let's go," he said, and held out his hand.

Chapter Seven

Jake sat at the edge of the bed, watching me dry myself with the huge white towel.

"You'd better count your towels before I leave," I warned him teasingly. "Something this fluffy and soft might find a way of disappearing."

"Are you talking about the towel or yourself?" he teased back. I snapped the towel at him and went to put on my underwear. It was gone.

"Where's...uh, where's my underwear?" I asked, looking around.

"Oh! I almost forgot," Jake said, pulling out a box from under the bed. "I meant to give this to you earlier."

I opened the box. My eyes widened.

It was lingerie, the most beautiful I'd ever seen. It wasn't too lacy or frilled. Instead, the black silk fabric of the bra was studded with small clear gems along the band. I pulled on the black panties and examined the bra closely before putting it on.

"Are these... these aren't diamonds?" I asked.

"No? Then I'll have to take it back. The saleswoman must have lied to me."

"They're diamonds? Who puts diamonds on underwear? You can't even see them!"

"I can see them," Jake said, looking pleased with himself. "And I'll see them again tonight when I take you out of your dress."

I flushed and clasped the bra around my chest, hooking the straps carefully over my shoulders.

"Now the dress," Jake said.

"You know, the way you're looking at me, I almost don't mind wearing a dress," I said, pulling the blue dress over my head. It shimmered delicately, slipping over my curves without catching anywhere. I eyed the heels next to the bed.

"You don't like dresses?"

"Well, not usually," I said, admiring myself in the mirror. "This one might make me change my mind though."

Jake had an eye for dresses. I wasn't sure how he'd done it, but he managed to find something that made me feel comfortable while still being classy. The cream kitten heels I slipped on were almost as comfortable as sneakers.

Almost.

"You're certainly different from any other girl I've ever known," Jake said. "You can finish up in the bathroom. I'll be waiting by the elevator."

Finish up? It wasn't until I went back into the bathroom that I realized what he meant. There was a hairbrush, and a box of brand new makeup. I tried to remember what Steph had done to get me all pretty for Jake's party, and by the time I was finished I felt like I had done okay. It wasn't a supermodel staring back at me in the mirror, but it was good enough.

I did a little twirl in the mirror, watching my dress flow over my ankles, and giggled.

"Oh, man," I said to myself. "You'd better not let anyone else know about this, or you'll never live it down."

***

In the elevator, Jake made me look down over the city before pressing the button to go down. My heart rose into my stomach, but that was nothing compared to the feeling when he slipped his hand through the slit of my dress, cupping my ass. I could feel his cock hard against the small of my back.

"Look out. Look out there."

The lights of New York City swam in my vision as he kissed the side of my neck. I trembled as his fingers slid farther, hooking their way under my panties.

"I'm already wet, if that's what you're wondering," I said. My voice was shaky.

"I want you wet. Always. I want you hot and wet and ready for me when I decide to take you."

When. Not if. *When*.

He had already chosen me. Why? I had no idea, but I didn't feel like pressing my luck with another snarky comment. I wasn't the old Lacey tonight. I was a girl in a dress on the arm of the richest, most handsome man in New York City, and I would act like it.

In front of the apartment, we waited only a few moments before a limousine pulled up to the curb. I gaped at Jake in disbelief.

"You're not telling me..." I trailed off. Jake opened the limousine door and held out a hand.

"It's not every night I get to take a beautiful woman out to dinner," he said.

I would have bet money that wasn't true. Jake Carville seemed like the kind of man who could take a different beautiful woman out to dinner every night for a year if he felt like it. But tonight, he had eyes only for me.

I decided to enjoy it. Inside of the limousine, Jake made me a cocktail from the built-in bar. He mixed gin, vermouth, anisette, and a pink liquor I couldn't identify immediately. He winked at me when he saw me watching.

"Well then, my little bartender, I'm sure you know what this is."

"Looks like a Peggy," I said. "If that's—"

"Dubonnet Rouge. Yes, it is. We always called it a Fever because of the blush."

"I've never heard that before," I said. His fingers brushed against mine as he handed over the cocktail.

"Sorry for assuming. Do you drink?" Jake asked teasingly.

"Only when I'm not working," I said, sipping at the cocktail.

"Good. You're more mature than women ten years older than you."

I bit my tongue. I wasn't mature at all, not sexually at least. And sitting next to Jake brought up all kinds of images of him teaching me all about sex. I shook my head and stared out of the window, catching his glance. *I want you to be hot and ready for me*, he'd said.

When we arrived at the restaurant, flashes of light came from the crowd on the sidewalk. Some of them seemed like professional cameramen.

"Wait here," Jake said, before I could open the door.

He came around and opened the door for me. I stepped out carefully, and his fingers pinched the slit of my dress together.

"Wouldn't want your underwear on the front of the tabloids tomorrow," he said.

Why was he so famous? Every detail he told me only led to further questions. If I'd had my phone, I would have looked him up. Right now, though, I was happy just to be at his side, living in a dream.

We went up the stairs to the restaurant. It was a Brazilian place situated just outside of Battery Park. The walls were trellises with flowered vines growing over them, and candles made the rooms dance with fire. It was a beautifully elegant setting.

As we sat down at the table, I looked out at the view to the west. The Statue of Liberty was lit up by a spotlight across the water.

"She looks so tiny from here," I said.

A man stopped at our table, staring at me strangely. I stared right back at him. Who was he, a waiter? No. He was blond and tall, the picture of a movie star. He looked vaguely familiar, but I couldn't place him. Then I heard Jake's voice boom out from behind.

"Lucas!"

I watched in confusion as Jake leaned over and clapped a hand to the man's shoulder. When he turned to me and introduced his friend, I realized how I'd heard the name before.

"Lucas. So you're the one who…" I didn't know how else to say it. He was the man who'd given another girl as a gift to Jake. What kind of a person did that, just

151

straight up bought another person for a week? It seemed oddly repulsive, although I suppose anyone could say that I was in the same position.

"This isn't the girl I sent you," Lucas said, his eyes narrowing.

"Lucas, Lucas. You always have such good taste. When I saw this beautiful young lady, I thought for certain that you had sent her. And by the time your actual gift came, I was already smitten."

Smitten. That was a word I hadn't heard except in romance novels. Jake's eyes were dancing with humor, though, and I thought he was joking. Surely he was joking.

"How did you two meet?" Lucas asked.

"Well," Jake said, giving my hand a squeeze on the table, "I saw her bare feet peeking out from a canvas in my art gallery."

"You broke into his art gallery?"

I flushed in shame.

"Well, I mean, I didn't break into it—"

"She was delivering a cake."

"A cake? How serendipitous."

"I told her the universe sent her to me."

"The universe is a better gift-giver than I am, apparently."

"Please, don't be offended."

"Of course not. I understand how you could get wrapped up in this girl's charms."

He looked at me. I had no idea what he was talking about. Charms? I was about as uncharming as a tomboy could be.

"Excuse me. I was about to use the restroom," Jake said, standing up. Lucas slipped into his seat as quickly as if they'd been playing musical chairs.

"I'll keep this lovely lady company until you're back."

"Don't let him steal you away," Jake said to me, coming around behind my chair. He kissed my shoulder and I felt a twinge of embarrassment at the public display of affection. "He's a rogue in sheep's clothing."

"I wouldn't dare take away one of your toys," Lucas said, leaning back in the chair. "You'd pitch a fit."

Jake lifted one finger in warning and stepped away from the table. When he was gone, Lucas grinned at me.

"Is that what I am?" I asked. "A toy?"

"Hasn't he played with you?" he asked.

I could feel the blood rushing to my cheeks.

"That's personal."

"I'm sorry. Really, I am. Now that you're blushing, though, I can see why Jake is attracted to you."

"Oh?"

"You seemed older before. Now, you look perfectly innocent."

My eyes flashed up to Lucas.

"Is that what he likes?"

"He likes… well, I'll let him tell you what he likes. He won't hold back, of that much I'm certain."

A boat went by, its motor humming, and we both watched as it went by.

"He hasn't told me much about himself," I said cautiously, after the boat had gone. "About his family or anything."

"His family?"

"Yes."

"Then you don't know—"

Lucas cut himself off and leaned over the table.

"What do you know about Jake Carville?" he asked.

"Nothing," I said, mystified at his reaction. "I just told you. We're just getting to know each other better. But he doesn't give too many answers to my questions."

"Well, here's one piece of advice. Don't ask about his family."

"Why not?"

"He doesn't have one. He's the Carville kid. Don't you remember?"

I shook my head. The phrase was familiar, somehow, but I couldn't put my finger on it.

"Anyway, it's a sore spot. He'll tell you about it, I'm sure. If he keeps you for a while."

I frowned. I hated how he spoke about me, as though I was an object to be picked up and then discarded.

"I can only hope he treats his toys well," I said, seething between my teeth. "I'm sure you treat all your gifts as nicely as you hope to be treated."

Lucas opened his mouth as though he was about to answer, but just then Jake returned from the bathroom. He'd been quick, and I didn't know whether it was because he didn't want to leave me alone with Lucas, or because he didn't want Lucas revealing any of his family secrets. Either way, Lucas stood up from the table.

"Sorry to leave you so soon," Lucas said. "Your lovely companion reminded me that I have somewhere to be."

"Such a shame you can't join us," Jake said teasingly. "We would have had such a romantic dinner, the three of us."

"Maybe some other time," Lucas said, winking at me. He stood up from the table and pushed the seat in behind Jake. "Pleasure to meet you."

"Same," I said, reminding myself to ask Jake about his family later.

Chapter Eight

I didn't want to sour the mood, so I avoided the topic of Jake's family. It wasn't hard. He asked me about my favorite artists, and he was surprisingly knowledgeable about contemporary art and the influences that had brought me all the way to New York City. I found myself nodding and leaning forward, anxious to hear what he thought about the newest installations in the contemporary art museum.

Silly. It was almost like we were on a date.

A waiter came by with a huge piece of meat skewered on a metal rod. He waited for me to speak, his eyebrows raised.

"Rump roast," the waiter prodded.

"Uh. Oh." I didn't know what to say.

"Yes, a few slices for the lady," Jake said. The waiter nodded and set the rod on the table. He deftly sliced through the meat. The juicy slices peeled off onto my plate, the meaty aroma wafting to my nostrils. My stomach gurgled.

After the waiter had served Jake, I whispered to him.

"What's that all about?"

"It's a churrascaria," Jake said.

"A chur-what?"

"A churascaria," he repeated. "They bring the meats out to your table and slice them fresh. You can have whichever ones you like."

"As much as I want?"

"Of course."

"Can I have one of all of them?"

Jake laughed.

"You might get stuffed before you know it. There'll be tri-tip and rack of lamb and duck and probably ten different kinds of pork."

"I want it all," I said primly, forking a bite of the meat into my mouth.

"You can have whatever you want," Jake said, the meaning heavy in his words.

I ate and ate and ate. Jake was right; by the time the fifth waiter had come around, I was stuffed. But I was determined to try at least a little bit of everything.

"I'm ready to become a vegetarian after this," I said.

"Don't you dare. There's a barbecue place near my apartment that has the most amazing ribs. To die for."

"I can't move."

"You have to. Come on, let's dance."

"Dance?"

"It'll settle all the meat down in your stomach and make room for dessert."

"Dessert?" I groaned but let him lead me onto the dance floor. A few older couples were already swaying to the four-piece string band.

The music was low and we didn't bother much in following the beat. My heart was pounding too hard to be able to hear the rhythm of the songs, anyway. Jake, too, seemed preoccupied, his fingers tapping against my waist impatiently.

I looked down and put a hand over his.

"What's the matter?" I asked.

"Nothing," he said. His green eyes refocused closer, looking deeply into my face. For the second time, I thought that he was looking a bit too deeply. I wondered what he saw in me that held his attention at all. I was just a young painter trying to make it. Girls like me were a dime a dozen. But it was me in his arms, rocking side to side, and when he pulled me close, I rested my head against his shoulder.

"Thank you for taking me out tonight," I said.

"It was my pleasure," Jake murmured, and he sounded utterly sincere. And after a year's worth of dates with guys who tried desperately to get me to come back to their apartments for sex, his sincerity was... strange. Not to mention the fact that this guy—this sincere, romantic man—had taken me without remorse when he thought I was a birthday gift.

Right then, though, it didn't matter. What mattered was the stars shining through the glass ceiling, the waves outside in the darkness, and the strong tall man holding me. I felt as though he was my gift from the universe, and I wasn't about to let him go.

He danced with me. In his arms, with the Statue of Liberty shining like a green beacon behind us, I felt utterly sated. I didn't want anything else. Only this.

Only him.

***

"Where are we going? My bedroom?"

"No."

"Your bedroom?"

"No."

He showed me down the hall. It was a locked door. Locked, just like the storage room in his art studio. He opened it, and I stepped inside.

Instantly the fuzziness in my mind dissipated.

"*Criminy.*"

"I don't think I've ever heard that word in here," Jake said.

I looked around. Unlike the other rooms in this house, this room was dimly lit and the walls were closer together. It felt tight. Claustrophobic.

In the middle of the room was a bed with ivory sheets, lit from above with a single spotlight. No pillows, though. Only four bedposts, from which dangled chains that ended in black velvet-covered cuffs. I swallowed.

Behind the bed was a huge mirror taking up the entire wall. As I stepped into the room, I saw my reflection staring back at me. It was strangely modern for an apartment that looked like Versailles.

The other walls weren't decorated the same as the rest of the house, either, I noticed, looking around. Instead of the classic oak paneling with gilt-frame oil paintings, the walls here were all concrete. Painted concrete.

Some of the artwork on the walls were words. Squinting, I could barely make them out. *SCREAM*, one of the walls read. Across from it, in equally imposing letters: *BREATHE.*

"What is this?"

"This is where I go to be myself."

"Who are you?"

He didn't answer me.

Over the words and around them were all kinds of abstract shapes. I stepped closer to the wall to see that the shapes were smaller, or made of smaller fragments of shapes. They looked like animals, almost, the way they were pieced together behind the words that splashed across the full walls. Small circles looked like eyes. Slits for mouths. Or maybe I was only imagining it.

"Pareidolia," I murmured.

"What did you say?"

"Pareidolia," I repeated, my fingers running down the walls. Every square inch was painted with something different. Another shape. Another animal. "You know, when you see faces when they aren't there. Like the man in the moon."

"Is that what you see?"

I started back at his touch. He'd come up just beside me and put his hand on my shoulder.

"I guess."

"What do you see when you look at me?" he asked.

I looked at him. His face wasn't well-lit, but I let my eyes trace down the lines of his eyebrows, his nose, his chin.

Emeralds.

No, not emeralds. Something less… elegant.

Uncut gems.

"I see the green in your eyes," I said. "Deep. The more I look, the darker they get."

Brilliant stones, raw and unpolished. Hidden in the depths of the earth, where fires burn.

"You see the darkness."

I didn't know what he wanted from me. Standing so close to me, he took my focus away from the art on the walls. His eyes...

Yes, the darkness.

I inhaled, aware that I had been holding my breath. It seemed to snap him out of his reverie.

"Come," he said. That one word, nothing more.

He took my wrist and led me to the bed that was in the middle of the room. I could feel his fingers burning on my skin, sending tingles of anticipation through me.

This was it. I steadied myself and stood ready. Ready, I thought, for whatever came next.

I wasn't ready, though. I wasn't ready at all.

"Jake?"

"Don't call me that," he said blankly.

"Sorry."

"Take off your dress."

There was a strange look in his eyes. A thrill went down my spine. He was going to take me. He was going to get me naked and then have sex with me and I would no longer be a virgin. The thought of it made my heart leap with fear and desire both.

I slipped off the straps of the dress. It puddled around my feet and I stepped out of it.

"Now your bra," he said.

He wasn't touching me, but it felt like the whole room had hands on me as I reached back and unclasped my bra. I wetted my bottom lip and let it fall to the floor.

He nodded, inhaling slightly.

"Your panties."

Jake inhaled slightly as I bent down and pushed down my panties to my ankles, stepping out one foot at a time.

He patted the middle of the bed and I crawled over. Naked, on my hands and knees, I had never felt so vulnerable.

First he took one of my hands. A vision popped into my head of him kissing the back of my hand like Prince Charming. It quickly evaporated as he lifted my arm and clicked one of the handcuffs securely around my wrist. Then another handcuff on the other wrist.

"You wanted to know who I am?" he said flatly. He pulled at the chains at the bedposts and my hands were yanked upward into the air. I yelped as the cuffs stretched my arms out wide. I was on my knees, in a grotesque imitation of Da Vinci's Vitruvian Man.

"This is who I am," he said. His voice had dropped to a low whisper, but in this room it sounded as loud as anything. My heart was pounding in my ears.

He let his suit jacket drop off of him, catching it with one hand. He tossed it over one of the bedposts and walked around behind me. I craned my head but couldn't see him anymore.

Crack! It was the sound of his hand on my ass that made me jump, before the tingles of pain shot across my skin. I cried out, and as my mouth opened he brought his tie around, gagging me with the fabric. I felt his fingers knot the tie roughly behind my head, and I whimpered.

All of a sudden, the weight of my decision, of my acceptance, came crashing down on me. I was tied up, and he was going to use me however he wanted. My breaths came fast through the gag, and I tried not to hyperventilate.

At the same time, his spank had woken up part of me that I didn't know existed. Heat surged through my body and a throb of desire made its way even through my fear.

"You're about to find out more about me than you might have wanted to know. You might find out something about yourself, too, Lacey," he whispered in my ear. I shuddered as he ran a finger down my spine. And I knew when he spoke, *knew*, without a shadow of a doubt, that he was smiling.

"Let's get started."

Chapter Nine

He ran his hand down my back, feeling everything. His hands moved down, over my hips, past where I was hot and throbbing. They moved down over my legs and my calves. His touch was a caress, but it was a possessive touch. As though he was examining a piece of property that he'd just bought. I supposed that was kind of true. He'd bought me with a few kind words and a decision.

No. There was something else about him. Something that I couldn't see now, but I knew was there. It was the way he'd looked at me in the art gallery. Underneath the Kage painting.

"When I first saw you, Lacey, do you know what I saw?"

I shook my head.

"I saw your feet. Barefoot. Vulnerable."

His hands moved now to the bare soles of my feet. I twitched as he cupped my foot in his hand, his thumb caressing the arch there.

"I thought that's what you would be. Just like all my others. Young and innocent."

He shifted his weight and now I could see him out of the corner of my eye. His hand reached around and cupped my breast.

"But you're more than that, aren't you, Lacey?"

I didn't know what he was talking about. I stared up at him baldly, unable to understand. Unable to speak, but even if the gag had fallen from my mouth I would have nothing to say.

"You want this without even knowing what you want. Your body screams for it."

He touched the inside of my thigh where it was wet. He brought his hand up and licked his fingers. My eyes widened.

"How have you gone this long without being touched?"

He trailed his hands down.

"Tonight, you're mine. I'll try to keep from ruining you… for as long as I can." His voice was hoarse, and I noticed the bulge in his pants, his hard breaths. His obvious arousal only made my heart beat faster.

He reached over and took hold of the chains. Suddenly the cuffs around my wrists gave way. The chains were loose. Was he letting me go?

"Touch yourself," he said. I looked up at him with wide eyes. I had never masturbated in front of anyone before.

"Will I have to punish you?" he asked. I shook my head quickly—no. My hands were already sliding into place, my fingers on both sides of my slit. I began to touch myself, slowly at first, then faster.

He was stroking himself through his pants, watching me. It should have felt dirty, but it was the most intimate thing I'd ever experienced.

"That's it. I want you to pleasure yourself, Lacey. Touch yourself the way you want me to touch you."

That was easier. I closed my eyes, imagining again his fingers inside of me. My own fingers began to stroke harder. I could feel the pressure inside of me rising.

I was surprised when he tore the gag from my mouth. My lips were dry, and I opened my eyes to see him in front of me.

God, I wanted him to kiss me. I leaned forward, my lips aching, but he shoved me back hard. I could see that it was just as hard for him to control himself, but he did. Beads of sweat stood out on his forehead as he pulled back.

"Please—" I managed to whisper.

"I want to hear you when you make yourself come," he said, his eyes blazing. I closed my eyes but I could still see him in front of me, his cock hard and visible through his pants. I touched myself and bit my lip as the throb of desire grew and grew.

In my childhood home, I'd learned to touch myself quietly. It was a habit I'd never gotten rid of. I suppose I never knew what men wanted in bed, but I'd seen a few clips of porn—enough to know that guys liked women who screamed. I didn't know how, though.

I was coming closer and closer to the edge, closer to the abyss. With my eyes closed, I could forget that he was watching me. Forget the strange room I was in, and the stranger circumstances that had led me to this place. A hard breath shuddered through me as my fingers worked into a furious rhythm.

Closer, closer, until—

"Ah!" I cried.

Jake had pulled the chains, tearing my hands away. A low breath shuddered out of my chest.

"Wh—why—"

Since spanking me, he'd done nothing but give me gentle caresses, so it startled me when he slapped me across my breasts hard.

"Were you going to come?"

I stared at him wildly. Desire contorted my body.

"You will tell me before you come," he said. He said it without malice, without scorn. He said it evenly, so calmly that I had to play back the words in my mind before they settled into understanding.

"Jake—"

Oh, God. I'd forgotten not to say his name. He was right in front of me then, his fingers pinching my nipples, twisting hard. Pain seared my nerves.

Still...

"Please, I'm sorry—"

He grabbed the chains, but instead of raising them again, he let them out completely. My wrists fell to my sides, the ties slack.

If I thought he was going to let me out so easily, though, I was mistaken.

He shoved me backwards and I fell onto my back. The breath I'd been holding went out of me with a gasp.

He leaned over to the side of the bed. I heard the jingle of the chain as he grabbed it. He moved it down, his face intent.

"What are you—"

"Hush."

"Are you going to punish me again?"

He moved to the other side of the bed and made the same motion. I tried to sit up to see what was going on, but he reached up quickly and grabbed the ends of the chains at the bedposts, pulling them.

With a sharp jerk, I realized what he'd done. The chains had been loose before, but now they were wound around something at the sides of the bed. When he pulled them tight, my arms were pulled outward instead of up.

And I was held fast against the bed.

"I hope that this isn't too much of a punishment for you, my innocent."

Jake was on his knees, his fingers unbuttoning his pants. My mouth went dry.

"I know you're a virgin," he said, taking off his shirt before shucking off his pants. He was wearing black briefs. I could see the clear outline of his cock throbbing behind the fabric. It cast a shadow that made the black fabric seem even darker. The intellectual part of my brain kept a running commentary.

Black on black, it said. *Notice the value of the color even in its absence. Shades, not tints. A black that is darker than itself where the light hasn't touched it. Not a true black, not yet, but close—*

I clamped down on that part of me as Jake shifted his weight, drawing nearer.

"Have you ever sucked cock, Lacey?" he asked. His voice was strong and bold, and mine came out as a squeak.

"No."

"Then this will be education, not punishment. Although, if you ever try to come again when I haven't told you to, I will punish you dearly. Understood?"

I nodded, but in all honesty he could have told me that he was going to draw and quarter me and I would have nodded. My eyes were fixed on the thick, throbbing outline. The darker black under the shadow of his cock. His thumb hooked into the waistline of his briefs.

"Good girl," he said, and my heart almost warmed at the compliment. "Let's begin."

Chapter Ten

Jake pulled down his briefs and his cock sprang out. My jaw clenched as I took in the thick length of it. His fingers stroked all the way down the shaft, and my eyes followed, taking in every detail.

I couldn't keep my eyes off of him as he stroked himself slowly. The skin on his cock was smooth except for a vein that pulsed with his heartbeat. His shaft was a gradient of tan to pink; the tip of his head gleamed with precum already.

I bit my lip and his cock jerked up with a twitch. He smiled.

"You know what to do to make me hard," he said. "My god, Lacey, you are beautiful. Those gorgeous lips… you're impossibly tempting."

Then why haven't you kissed me? The thought rose and I shut it down. What was I asking for, sweetness? Romance? That wasn't why he wanted me, and it wasn't why I wanted him. At least, I didn't think so.

He wasn't even touching me, and yet I felt myself growing hot and aching again between my legs. Just looking at his cock sent all sorts of imagined feelings through my body. How it would feel as he pushed up into me for the first time. I couldn't imagine that he would fit all the way.

Now he straddled my chest, leaning over me, and I could see him up close. I smelled his musk, dark and rich.

There was a lighter scent too that must have been his soap, an airy smell that I thought the ocean must smell like in places that weren't New York City.

His hands rested on the bed above my head, tilting me back slightly with the indentation he made on the bed. Above me, inches from my face, his cock throbbed.

It was curiosity, curiosity more than anything, that made me stretch my neck to kiss him on his tip. The bead of precum smeared onto my lips and I slipped my tongue out to taste it gingerly, unsure of what I would find.

It was almost tasteless, slick on my tongue, and the finding gave me courage to kiss him again on his head. My lips parted and I let my tongue swirl around the impossible smooth mushroom tip. He groaned. His stomach caved inward with his breath as I sucked lightly and then let my head fall back against the soft bed.

"Jesus, Lacey," he said. His face was redder, whether because he was leaning so far over or because of my kiss I didn't know. "Don't stop."

He bent his knees further and then his cock was at my lips, urging itself into my mouth. I opened my mouth slightly and choked as he thrust himself inside halfway.

Panic seized me. My hands tugged at the chains on either side of me. I was choking, choking on his huge cock, and there was nothing I could do about it. His shaft was rock hard, hard as I never imagined a penis could be. I'd always thought that they would be somewhat flexible, like rubber. Like a hot dog. But Jake's cock was like steel inside my mouth. He shifted down, jamming his cock to the back of my throat.

When he finally pulled back, I gasped. Tears sprang to my eyes.

He reached back and slid his hand between my legs. To my surprise, he found me slick.

"You like that, my sweet girl?" he asked.

I couldn't answer him. My body had reacted with shock, yes, but also desire. I wanted more, though, from him. I needed more.

Before I could find the words, he was back again, easing his thick shaft along my lips without forcing himself inside. I gratefully licked and sucked at the underside of his shaft. I could feel the throb of his heartbeat quick against my tongue where the vein pulsed. It made my whole body shiver.

I'm doing this to him.

It was a feeling of incredible power, and before he could push himself into my mouth again I had already moved my head to take him in. I sucked and swallowed, wanting the invasion, wanting him to choke me with his thickness.

"God, Lacey," he hissed through his teeth. My name, uttered in his voice, sent a tremble through me and I swallowed again, forcing him to come deeper into me. I felt myself about to gag and I closed my eyes, willing my throat to relax. He stilled above me, the only motion the insistent throb of blood inside of him.

I began to bob my head slowly, my tongue moving along his shaft. The skin there was smooth, so smooth, covering his rock-hard erection. Soft and hard at the same time.

He moaned, and his hips began to rock slightly, sliding his cock in and out. I let my mouth loosen as he thrust forward, taking him as far as I could, letting my tongue lap against his underside.

"Oh God," he cried. His hands gripped my head, and I felt him tugging at my hair.

I pushed forward and heard him gasp. It made my own body ache for him. It felt so good to give him this pleasure, after all of the pleasure he'd given me. More than that, it made me feel powerful. The only thing I could control here was how much I gave him. And, Lord, despite everything that he'd done to me, I wanted to give him everything.

"Lacey, I'm coming. I'm going to—"

I swallowed again as his cock pulsed, thrusting against the back of my throat. His hot cum, salty and rich, filled my mouth. I swallowed, my tongue licking off all I could. He shuddered, his fingers tangled in my hair.

I wanted to give him everything. God, I wanted to give him *me*.

***

Jake collapsed at my side, his chest heaving. His fingers were still threaded through my hair and he caressed me slowly, absently.

"J—" I caught myself before I could use his name, then frowned. "I don't know what I should call you," I said.

"You don't need to call me anything," he said, but his face looked doubtful. I caught the worry in his eyes and then it disappeared, replaced by a blank calmness.

"Was it… did I do okay?"

"More than okay," Jake said, brushing strands of my hair back and staring deeply into my eyes. "God, Lacey, you're perfect."

I blushed. I was cuffed, chained to a bed, and I blushed like a little schoolgirl who'd just gotten her braids pulled by the boy she had a crush on.

If I hadn't been tied, I would have put my arms around Jake's neck, squirmed close to him. I suppose that's part of why he'd tied me up.

He sat up at the edge of the bed. His spine curved in a slow line all the way to his neck. The planes of his back muscles tensed as he put his hands on his knees.

I couldn't see his face, but then I remembered the mirror. Slowly, without shifting my weight, I bent my head back so I could see.

I saw myself, my hair a tangled mess, my arms to either side. My nipples were points against the darkness of the room. I saw the mussed sheets, the painted walls, the chains swinging slow arcs from the bedposts.

And I saw him.

His face contorted, and as he bent his head I saw—

No, no, I couldn't have seen that, I must be seeing things—

I saw a tear roll down his cheek. He brushed it away quickly with his finger, wiped his hand on the sheet. Then he looked in the mirror.

A noise rose from his throat. A choked growl, like a wounded animal. He spun, his eyes wild.

175

After all of the crazy things he'd done to me, I thought that he would never be able to scare me again. But this—this look in his eyes, this vulnerable anger—this terrified me like nothing else.

I wanted to reach out to him, but my arms were tied. I wanted to speak his name—Jake—but it died on my lips. He hated his name and I had nothing else to call him.

"Please," I said instead. "I'm sorry."

I didn't know what I was apologizing for, only that there was hurt in his face and I had been the one to hurt him, somehow.

He didn't respond. He yanked the edge of the sheet from the bed and threw it over me. He was at the door of the room before he looked back at me. He was only a silhouette against the light of the hallway.

"Sleep," he said finally. "I'll be back later."

With that, he turned off the lights and left me chained in the darkness.

***

HIS GIFT: PART THREE

A DARK BILLIONAIRE ROMANCE

Chapter One

I woke up to the sound of chains clinking against the bedposts.

Dreams from last night were swirling through my head. The paintings I'd done, the mindblowing orgasms I'd received from an expert tongue between my legs. Jake Carville, billionaire, tying me down naked to a bed and choking me with his huge cock.

Jake.

I opened my eyes. He was unhooking the chains from the sides of the bed. He looked like he'd just stepped out of a business meeting—his white shirt was crisp and clean, and he'd put on a new suit, one that wasn't stained with paint. He looked down at my body and smiled slowly, his jaw dark from where he hadn't bothered to shave. And I...

I was still naked.

It hadn't been a dream.

"Good morning," he said.

"Good morning."

I didn't talk about what had happened last night, but in my mind all I could see was the single tear rolling down his cheek. I'd failed him somehow, but I didn't know what I'd done or not done.

He still hadn't kissed me. Still hadn't taken my virginity. Now, I didn't know if he ever would. He studiously avoided my eyes as he took a small key from his jacket pocket and unclasped the cuffs around my wrists.

"How are you feeling today?"

Fine. Just fine. My arms are just fine after being chained up all night. And I didn't even get to brush my teeth after giving you a blowjob, but hey, whatever, I'm fine.

"I'm okay," I said warily.

I stretched my arms after he uncuffed me, rolling my shoulders. All things considered, I felt great. He must have let me sleep in.

"Only okay?"

"Well, I—ah!"

I yelped as he pushed my shoulders back, pinning me down against the bed.

"We can't have that, can we now?" Jake murmured. "I don't want you to feel okay, Lacey."

His hands were moving fast, cupping my breast. He squeezed a yelp out of me.

"I want you to feel positively *delightful.*"

With that, he dove down and licked me. One swipe of his tongue was all it took to send my body arching against the bed. Thrills ran through my nerve endings as he kissed and sucked me. I squirmed as his tongue worked wonders between my legs, my breaths coming harder and faster.

"You're a good girl, Lacey," he breathed. I moaned as his fingers found my nipple and twisted it, sending a shock of heat through my chest. His other hand massaged underneath me, kneading my asscheek.

"*Yes,*" I breathed.

"I want you to come for me. Quickly, now," he said. "We don't have much time."

"Much time for what—oh!"

He'd bent his head and sucked hard, and I clenched my eyes, bucking against his mouth. My hands moved wildly over his back, threading through his hair. I gripped him close to the scalp as he pulled me up to his mouth, laving my now-swollen clit urgently with his tongue.

I'd gone from being asleep to being wide awake. Now, as he worked me over with his tongue, I moaned and clenched my eyes. The spark of desire that had woken up with me was fanned into full flame, and inside of my chest I burned to climax. *Come for me,* he'd said, and I was already most of the way there. The pressure built and built as his tongue slipped in quick rhythm over my aching slit.

"I know how to make you come," he said. The hand that had moved underneath me now slipped between my thigh, and I groaned as he thrust his fingers into me. His fingers stretched me, and the delicious friction from his thumb made me cry aloud.

"Oh God," I moaned. "Oh yes. Yes. Yes, please—"

He thrust his fingers into me at the same rhythm as his tongue. His lips burned hot at my entrance and when he sucked me, the pressure threatened to burst me into pieces. I cried aloud as he pushed me faster, faster, sending shocks through my body with every thrust of his fingers.

"Now, Lacey," he said, and the suction from his lips pulsed at the same frenetic pace as his fingers. I gripped his shoulder with one hand and the sheets with the other, lifting my hips to meet him.

"Oh God," I said. "*OH, OH, OHHH!*"

The force of the orgasm shuddered me in thick, rippling waves. I screamed, arching my head back against the sheets. It had come so quickly, but it stayed for what seemed like hours. Light exploded through my body, and I writhed as his fingers plunged into me over and over again, sending new waves of pleasure through me.

Yesterday, he'd lavished attention on me even after my orgasm, licking and sucking sweetly at me. Now, it seemed like he had no time for anything else. He sat up, a smile of satisfaction on his face, and wiped his mouth with a handkerchief. He gently wiped my juices from where they'd smeared down the inside of my leg.

I panted, breathless, and let my head fall back onto the bed. The force of the orgasm had knocked me so hard that I saw black spots in front of my eyes. My heart was pounding.

"What a wakeup call," I said.

"Get up," Jake said.

"Now? Can't I take a second and—"

"Get up."

Sighing, I rolled over and sat up. My knees were shaky, and I leaned back on my hands.

"Wrap that sheet around yourself."

"Sure," I said, obeying his command. You couldn't *not* obey that voice. It spoke low and hard, and when he told me to do something there was no hint of a doubt that I would actually do it.

The sheet was silk and hard to keep up, so I knotted it in a clumsy knot on one side under my armpit. It hung low, exposing most of my butt, but it was the best I could do.

The thought that I'd woken up with struck me again. Even as I caught my breath, I looked up at Jake to judge whether or not this would be a good time to bring it up.

"Can we… can we talk about last night?" I asked. There was a lump in my throat, but I swallowed it.

"Later," he said.

"Okay, but I just want to know—"

"Later." His voice was tinted with irritation, and I got the feeling that nobody around him ever pressured him to do anything.

"Look, if you don't want to talk to me, you might as well toss me out on my ass now. I don't know why you want to put it off—"

"The police."

His voice was calm, but the words he said made me stop cold.

"Excuse me?"

"The police are here," Jake said, as calmly as he'd said good morning. "And they want to talk to you."

Chapter Two

I don't know what I was expecting, but when Jake ushered me into the hallway my heart stopped. Two policemen were standing in the hall.

I couldn't have turned redder if I'd been hit in the face with an iron after running a marathon. There I was, in nothing more than a *sheet*, my hair mussed and my teeth unbrushed. I gaped at them.

Both men looked me up and down, surprise written all over their faces. One of them was a head shorter than the other, and he smirked at me with a stupid presumptuous grin.

"Here she is, gentlemen," Jake said smoothly. His arm came around my waist. I wanted to shake him off. Heck, I wanted to punch him in the gut and ask him what he thought, parading me out in one of his bedsheets like I was a piece of evidence in a court case.

"You're—ah, you're Lacey Mills?" the taller officer said.

"Um, y-yeah," I stammered. I rubbed the sleep out of my eyes. This wasn't happening. I was standing half-naked in a hallway with two cops questioning me, and my bare ass hanging out of the sheet that didn't do anything to cover my obviously protruding nipples.

"We received a call from a Stephanie, ah—what was her name?" the officer said, flipping through his notebook.

"Hart," I said, at the same time as the shorter officer. He leered at me again, obviously having a lot of fun interrogating me. A billionaire's lay for the night.

"Yeah, Hart. She said you'd gone missing and you might be here."

"Called a half dozen times before you'd even been gone twenty-four hours," the short guy said, crossing his arms.

"Hmm," I said noncommittally. That sounded like Steph. She'd joked that she would give me a week to be kidnapped, but she'd probably gotten worried the second I hadn't called her to let her know what had happened.

"As you can see, there's obviously been a misunderstanding," Jake said. His hand slipped lower, cupping my ass. I bit my lip and tried not to squeal as his fingers moved along my curves.

"Yeah, sure, sure. Miss, are you here of your own free volition?"

"Free what?"

"He's not locking you up here against your will?"

I flushed, thinking about Jake tying me to the bed. As he squeezed my asscheek, I shook my head frantically.

"No, no," I said. "Not at all."

"Good. You call your friend, tell her you're alright," the taller officer said, closing his notebook. "So she stops calling the station every ten minutes for an update."

"I w—I will," I said, my words jerking as Jake's hand slid between my thighs, one finger curling upward into me. The officer narrowed his eyes at me, then sniffed.

"Thank you for your time, officers," Jake said, so coolly I almost couldn't believe he had one finger sliding under my folds.

The policemen nodded and walked back down the hall.

***

I turned and smacked Jake on the shoulder as soon as the policemen had disappeared into the elevator.

"Ow! What the hell?" He gripped his shoulder like I'd actually hurt him.

"That's what I should be saying! Is this how you thank me for last night's blowjob? By parading me half naked around armed policemen?"

"I didn't notice they were armed," Jake said, smiling, "but I don't think they were planning to take you down."

"I have to call Steph," I said. "And let her know that I'm okay." My mind was slowly gaining its sanity back. Policemen? Jeez Louise. What a way to wake up in the morning.

"It's nice of your friends to check up on you," Jake said.

"Yeah. I have great friends. They don't buy me sexy men as birthday presents or walk around with collars on at my parties, but they're okay people, all things considered."

Jake's grin spread wider.

"There's a phone in your bedroom at the end of the hall," he said. "You can call her from there."

"Great," I said, storming off in the direction he pointed. "Wait. *My* bedroom?" He was giving me a bedroom?

"And tell her not to call the police again, but that you won't be around for the rest of the week," he called.

I froze in the hallway. My bare feet sank into the plush carpet and I leaned one hand against the wall. Jake's glorious green eyes glittered at me as I shot his question back to him.

"Oh, I won't?"

"No," he said, as though it was the most obvious thing in the world. "You're staying here."

Chapter Three

In keeping with the overall vintage castle feel of the place, the phone in my room was an old brass rotary phone. I had to spin the circular panel in front to dial Steph's number. It took me four times to get it right; I kept fumbling and the thing spun the wrong number, but finally I got through.

"Steph?"

"Lacey! You're okay!"

"Yeah, I'm fine. More than fine, actually." I stretched one arm over my head and lay back onto the soft covers of the bed.

"You sound like you just got head from a sexy billionaire."

I choked, and then tried to cough to get the lump out of my throat, then choked again. On the other end of the line, I heard Steph squeal.

"Oh my God! Andy totally called it. Andy, you were right!"

"Jeez, Steph—"

"Tell me all about it."

"I can't. Look, Steph, I just had to talk to two policemen in nothing but a sheet, and it's all your fault."

"What's the guy's name?"

"You made his birthday cake, Steph. You don't know his name?"

"Psshh," she said. "It's not like it said *Happy Birthday Eustace* or whatever on it. It was gold orchids—"

"Not Eustace. Ugh, what kind of a name is that, anyway?"

"A billionaire name."

"I'd never fall for someone named Eustace, even if he was a billionaire. Okay, Steph, I'll tell you all about him later," I said. For some reason I was unsure how much I wanted to tell Steph. She probably knew the name Jake Carville, at least if he was as famous as I thought he was. And as curious as I was to know his background... I wanted him to be the one to tell me. Was that weird?

"One little detail. One more. Please."

"Okay, fine," I said, racking my brain. "His penthouse apartment has an art gallery inside of it. That's where we met, and he kind of... uh... went crazy with putting his hands all over me." And inside of me, too. But I knew Steph would freak out if she heard that.

"Oh. My. God."

"Yeah, and he has this art studio too. It's amazing. He let me paint on all these canvases, and he's got these oils—"

"Lacey, please. Focus. Less about paint. More about the sexy man who put his tongue in your pink."

I blushed to think about it.

"He's got beautiful green eyes, and dark hair, and he—oh, Steph! We kind of... well, he kind of... ripped your dress. I'll buy you a new one—"

That was all I got out, because both Steph and Andy were hooting with laughter on the other end of the line.

"So you're not a virgin anymore, huh? We're going to have to celebrate with champagne once you get out."

"Yeah, uh, well…"

"Well what?"

I twisted my fingers in the sheets as I stared up at the ceiling.

"Well technically I'm still a virgin. I guess. Technically."

"He didn't fuck you?"

"No," I admitted.

"Why not?"

"Look, I don't know. He's… well, he's kind of a strange guy. Secretive."

My thoughts drifted to the black door in the art studio. Storage, he'd said. But if that's all it was, why was he so adamant about keeping me out of there?

"Maybe he's a eunuch."

"No, he definitely—ah, he definitely has a dick." I coughed, thinking about the way his cock had thrust against the back of my throat.

"AHHH!" Andy was screaming into the phone. "I want to know all about it! Is he big? Does he have a gay friend? Lacey? Lacey—"

"Sorry about that," Steph said, having evidently wrenched the phone back from her brother. "You are going to give me the full lowdown when you get back. Got it?"

I pinched the bridge of my nose. I didn't know how girls talked about sex like this with each other. Thinking about all of the things Jake had done to me made me squirm with anticipation. I didn't want to hold anything back from my best friend, but I wasn't about to give her a play by play recap of everything Jake had done to me.

"Sure thing, Steph," I said. "Um, and just to let you know, so you don't send any more police officers after me, I'm going to be here for a while."

"What?"

"Like, another week. He asked me to—"

I was cut off by Steph's squeal, so loud that I think it might have broken the rotary phone speaker.

"Steph? Hello?"

"You have a sexy billionaire dude in *love* with you and you didn't tell me?"

"He's not in love with me. He just—"

"He wants you to stay in his place for a whole week? Are you freaking kidding me? Andy, are you hearing this?"

"Steph, look, I've got to go."

"You have to go get fucked by your gorgeous billionaire's huge cock, right, right. Gotcha. I expect a full report."

"Sure," I said, because it was easier than saying no. I told Steph to let everyone at my work know that I was sick for the week, both because I really didn't want to have those conversations with my bosses, and also because, well, I didn't remember their phone numbers and I couldn't very well look anything up on a rotary phone.

When I hung up on her, I lay back against the soft cushions and looked around my bedroom.

My bedroom.

I wondered if Jake really wanted me the way Steph thought he might. In love? No, definitely not. He hadn't even kissed me on the mouth. If he wanted me, he only wanted me for sex. And yet, he hadn't taken my virginity yet. He hadn't told me any of the secrets about his family that apparently everybody but me knew about.

I would have to ask him. When the time was right. I would ask him, and I would see what Jake Carville really wanted with me.

***

I took another bath. The darned tub didn't even have a showerhead.

"Darn billionaires. Forcing me to bathe in leisure," I mumbled. I turned on the faucets and began to fill the tub.

I was only wearing a sheet, so I dropped it to the ground and stared at the wall-sized mirror in front of me. I frowned.

I didn't know what Jake Carville saw in me. He was a drop-dead gorgeous, wealthy as sin, completely in control individual. And me...

I was all curves and frizzed out hair. I tried to straighten down my bedhead, but to no avail.

Stop thinking about it.

I dropped my gaze from the mirror. It reminded me of the mirror in the room Jake had tied me up in. What a strange place, in the middle of this luxurious penthouse. It was so different from all of the other rooms in here. My bedroom was decorated in the same old-money style as the rest of the penthouse, but secretly I preferred the concrete walls painted with art.

That room is for sex.

But it wasn't. Or at least, it wasn't for sex with me. Maybe Jake was having sex with all of his other supermodels in there, but he wasn't having it with me. Was it that stupid idea of purity, of innocence? I hated that he only thought of me that way. I wasn't some stupid little naive girl. And just because I was still a virgin didn't mean I was devoid of sexual urges.

Oof. I stepped into the water and immediately thought of Jake's hands caressing me. Immediately my body burned hotter than the steaming water that I was sinking into.

God, his hands. His strong hands, sliding between my thighs—

Without thinking about it, my own hand drifted down to where he had touched me before. He hadn't let me come to orgasm then, but that didn't mean I couldn't now. And the idea of masturbating alone, without Jake there to witness, was more than tempting.

I began to slide my fingers over myself casually, as though I wasn't doing anything at all. I closed my eyes, expecting to see Jake. But instead—

The painting.

In my mind the Kage painting in Jake's gallery loomed large. I had been looking at it right before—

Before he touched me, my body said. Before he grabbed me and kissed my neck—

The lines of his letters, green and gold—

Like Jake's eyes, burning into mine. His fingers, hooking the hem of my dress and lifting it—

My fingers moved with an ever increasing rhythm under the water.

Back in Iowa, I'd touched myself as quietly as possible. When I came, I stuffed my face into a pillow and muffled the scream. Here, though, every little sigh of mine echoed in the bathroom. At first it startled me, but then I began to enjoy being able to be loud.

"Ohh," I moaned softly. My hands moved frantically between my legs, and my body ached for release. I closed my eyes, and again—

Kage, each letter a curling line intertwined with the others—

Jake, his lips hot on my neck, his finger thrusting into me—

I caught myself sliding down into the tub. My toes curled, pressed into the obsidian. I twisted, needing more—

Needing him—

And then I came, the climax fading as soon as it had arrived. I slumped back against the tub, breathing hard, the water steaming white like I was outside in winter. Even though I'd brought myself to orgasm, it wasn't enough. I felt like there was something missing—

Jake, his eyes green and gold—

And I couldn't figure out what it was I wanted. Frustrated, I splashed water over the sides of the tub.

"Argh!" I cried. I stood up then, letting the water drip down my body and puddle on the tile as I walked out of the bathroom. I didn't want to look at myself. I didn't want to ask myself questions that I couldn't answer.

In the privacy of my bedroom, I yanked open the dresser drawers. There was lingerie laid out for me, all in my size. I wondered idly if he kept all sizes. Maybe next week he would have to pull out the size zero dresses and the B-cup bras. The thought stabbed like a physical pain through my chest. I grabbed the plainest looking bra and panty set and slammed the drawer shut.

Why was I doing this to myself? Before I'd talked with Steph, things had been so simple. I would go along with Jake's orders, and that was all. Now, I was struggling to think about whether or not he wanted me, about whether he was regretting asking me to stay at all. I cringed to think about what would happen next week when I left.

"You're not his girlfriend," I said through gritted teeth. "You're not even his escort. All you are is a playtoy. A playtoy with a check for a year's worth of rent. So don't go messing it up by getting all emotional."

Steph said he was in love with you.

I growled at myself and turned to open the closet. He had bought me clothes. Not just any kind of clothes, though. I tore through the hangers, anger bubbling up inside of me.

Dresses.

All dresses.

I sighed. I would rather be naked than wear dresses. Maybe that's what he was counting on. I opened the dresser drawers. There was nothing inside but lingerie. Back to the closet. The only other thing there was a terrycloth robe.

"You want to give me dresses to wear?" I said, talking to myself as I pulled the robe out of the drawer and shrugged it on. "Fine. I'll figure something else out."

It was definitely more comfortable than a dress. And yet, when I left the bedroom, I felt a twinge of guilt. Should I dress up for him? He had given me a selection to choose from, after all. Would he be upset if I didn't want to wear them?

"Oh for God's sake," I said, snapping myself out of my thoughts. "He can darn well order me to wear a dress, if it's that important to him."

And for a brief moment, I thought that I would be happy if he gave me that order.

Chapter Four

By the time I got out of the bedroom, my stomach was growling. I looked forward to having another leisurely meal with Jake. Chocolate chip pancakes, maybe. We could sit and talk, and maybe I would ask him about that storage room, or about his family.

But it wasn't to be.

When I ventured out into the hallway, I heard plates clinking. I wandered down the hall, following the aroma of coffee to a kitchen. I pulled the robe around me, tying it tightly. I thought that Jake might pull the tie open. He might take my robe off—

"Shut up, Lacey," I said. "It's enough that he'll be here with you. Don't get stupid over him."

The breakfast table had been set out perfectly. The tablecloth was a shimmering ivory, and two plates had been laid out with napkins folded carefully on each one. A glass carafe of orange juice sat next to the silver pot of coffee. Stacks of pancakes filled a serving tray, and another tray heaped over with eggs and bacon. And in the middle of the table, a branch of orchids was arranged casually in a black ceramic vase. It was a work of art.

I breathed in the aroma and walked into the room just as Jake walked in from the opposite side. I opened my mouth to say good morning, but he beat me to it.

"I can't stay," Jake said.

My jaw snapped shut audibly, and my mind shut down along with it. I had been preparing all of my questions for him, but now that he'd thrown me off course I couldn't think of any response.

"Wh…What do you mean?"

He only raised one eyebrow. I pulled the robe tighter around me, and stammered as I leaned against the table. *Come on Lacey, what are you going to do, faint?*

"I thought… I thought we were going to talk and, you know, have breakfast together."

"Some of us have work to do today," Jake said, coming around the table. I waited none too hopefully for a kiss, but instead he slapped my ass and continued on to the hallway without missing a stride.

Okay, the romantic vibe was definitely gone. I turned around, irritation flushing my cheeks.

"Hey! What about me? You said that I couldn't go back to work!"

"You can paint, you can read, you can relax," Jake said. "Nothing more."

"Oh, I have to stay home like an invalid while you go do important man things?" I gestured out towards the city skyline.

"That's right."

"That's hypocritical!"

He didn't bother to argue with me. He only picked up his jacket from the coatrack and shrugged it on.

"I'll see you tonight," he said. "Remember: paint, read, relax. You're not allowed to leave."

"Maybe I'll call the police and tell them that Jake Carville kidnapped me," I said, crossing my arms and following him to the elevator door.

"Then Officers Tweedle Dum and Tweedle Dee will come get you, and you can go back to painting A-line cars," Jake said.

I frowned. He was right. Another day of painting was well worth being held captive in a penthouse. Even if it wasn't what I'd hoped for.

"I'm sorry we can't spend all morning getting to know each other," Jake said, the sarcasm so evident in his words that I hated myself for even thinking that we would have another romantic breakfast. He wasn't keeping me around to be a girlfriend, I reminded myself.

"I'll just eat all these pancakes for myself," I said, plopping down at the head of the table with an attitude I hoped looked like I didn't even care if he stayed or not. I loosened my robe. These pancakes were all mine, and I was taking no prisoners.

"Good," Jake said, smiling warmly. I could feel my heart melting under his smile, and I shook myself off to harden up. He didn't care about me, not really. I shouldn't care about him.

"Will you be a good girl while I'm gone?" he said.

"Depends on what you define as good."

"How about this: just keep the painting inside of the art studio and not on any of the living room walls."

"I'm not sure I can agree to that," I said jokingly. "That main window looks like it would make an excellent stained glass piece."

"Do I need to lock you up before I go?" Jake teased.

"No," I said, but I tried to pout.

He bent down to me, and before I knew it he'd hooked his finger into my bra, pulling it down. His mouth took my nipple, sucking it hard and sending electric thrills through my body. I gasped as he stood back up.

"And if you're a good girl, you'll have that to look forward to tonight. Understood?"

I breathed in sharply, unable to speak for a moment because of the insane desire that made me want to shove Jake Carville against the door instead of waiting patiently for tonight. Then I forced myself to nod.

"Yes," I said. "Understood."

***

Home alone. Hmm. I finished breakfast and did the dishes, even though I was pretty sure he had one servant to wash and one servant to dry. I wasn't about to leave his place a mess.

And what a place!

I poked around the house for a bit to see how a billionaire lived. The rooms were all elaborately decorated with the same kind of style, and I actually got bored wandering from one perfectly styled bedroom to the next. The room where he'd tied me up was locked up securely, and none of the rooms were all that interesting, except for the art gallery.

I spent an hour or so perusing all of the paintings there. A half hour to go through them all once, and another half hour to see if there was anything I'd missed.

All of the artists I knew said that they could spend hours staring at a single painting, but I was always too impatient for that. Still, I was glad that I went back through the gallery again, because if not, I would have missed it.

One of the smaller paintings that I hadn't noticed that first night caught my eye. The painting was stylized, abstract enough that you couldn't tell right away what the image was.

I had to step closer, almost put my nose up to it, to tell what the painter was going for. It was a woman, or at least a curved body that I thought was a woman. The features of her face were blurred out so that I couldn't see the expression. And her arms were strange, elongated, with lines extending from the ends of her hands. I couldn't tell exactly what it was, until...

There.

When I saw it, I took a step back in surprise. I hadn't recognized the shape because of the lines, but I knew now exactly what they were. The silver lines emanating from the palms, looking for all the world like energy beams coming out of a superhero's hands—they weren't lines at all.

They were chains.

The woman was tied up in the room that Jake had tied me up in. And again, I winced with jealousy. This was obviously a painting that Jake had either done himself or had commissioned, with a model who'd been in the same position I'd been in all last night. I frowned and turned away to look at another Kage painting.

Man, there were a lot of them.

The Kage paintings were just as prominent as ever. Indeed, the canvas that I'd been looking at the night of the party had a spotlight all to itself. It shone in the middle of the room.

At first I'd thought it had been a reproduction of one of Kage's pieces. A giclee print, maybe, like the kind you see hanging all over high-end galleries in the West End. But as I came closer, I realized that this wasn't a print. It was an original.

The paint was applied in thick strokes. I reached out to touch it. The drips were bumpy on the canvas. I squinted at the dripped paint. How had Jake managed to get this? How had he even gotten in contact with the most infamous street artist in New York City?

I turned away from the canvas. Jake Carville was a man full of mysteries. But there was one thing I knew: he had an art studio full of blank canvases, and I meant to paint them.

Chapter Five

It was six o'clock in the evening when Jake came back. I was in the art studio, busy with my painting. I'd managed to finish thirteen pieces. Two others were pushed to the side, half-done. They irritated me like I was a kid with a loose tooth ready to come out. I tongued them but couldn't figure out how to get rid of the idea in my head. They weren't quite right.

I was busy working on my fourteenth canvas when Jake arrived.

"What did you eat for lunch?"

"Lunch? Oh, right," I said. I looked out the window, where the sky was growing darker. "Lunch. What time is it?"

"It's dinnertime."

"Oh. Dang. Well, I got distracted." I dabbed another bit of blue onto the canvas. Not quite there, but close. I dabbed again.

"I can see that," Jake said.

"I'll be out in a sec," I said, dabbing again with a lighter tint of blue. "I need to finish—"

"Your painting? You've finished a lot of them already, I see."

Before I could protest, he stepped into the room. He moved among my paintings, studying them. Distracted, I swished my brush in the water to clean it. I could finish this painting later. Now…

Now, Jake was seeing my work.

I found myself holding my breath, hoping that he would say something about them to me. Even if he hated them… I wanted to know. I don't know why. He had good taste, I suppose, or similar taste. I wanted to know if he approved, or if he thought I was wasting his paint and his canvases.

I'd wasted a heck of a lot of them, after all.

"Would you like to go out to eat?" he asked, turning abruptly on his heel.

My shoulders slumped. The dark dread that had been building inside of me as he went from painting to painting descended on my head.

"What is it?" he asked. He tilted his head curiously at me. I sighed and gestured toward the canvases he had just looked at.

"Do you… I mean… what do you think?"

"I think you should have eaten lunch six hours ago."

"No," I said, hating the whining tone slipping into my voice. "I mean the paintings."

Jake couldn't hide the small smile at the corner of his lips.

"Do you care what I think about them?"

"Sure," I said.

"You shouldn't."

My lips parted in surprise.

"Why… why not?"

Jake squatted down in front of one of the canvases. He tilted it back so that the light hit it. Immediately I saw a line that I wanted to change, and

206

winced. Seeing me, he put the canvas down. He shook his head. I didn't know why, but I thought he looked at me with something like pity. Then it was gone as quickly as it had come. He stood up and held his arms open wide.

"Your art is for you. What I think about your paintings has nothing to do with the paintings. What if I told you they were all garbage, that you should burn them?"

My chest tightened.

"I don't... I mean, they're not that bad, are they?"

Jake stepped toward me, a smile spreading on his face.

"What if I told you I wanted to buy them? All of them? Five thousand dollars apiece."

"What? That's way too much!" I cried, gripping the paintbrush in my hands.

"See?"

Jake reached out to me and cradled my face in one hand. For a moment I thought he might... but no. He wouldn't kiss me. He turned and gestured back idly at the canvases.

"These are yours. Yours alone. Don't ever let anyone judge them."

He gave me a quick kiss on the forehead.

"Now go wash up for dinner. Get dressed in something that's not one of these damn robes. They're too tempting."

I was glad that he was still tempted by me, or at least willing to lie to me about it. But I wasn't about to let him have the upper hand just yet.

"All you have is dresses—"

"Wear a dress. And no panties. Understood?"

I stared baldly at him before giving up. If he wanted me in a dress, I'd have to wear a dress.

"Understood," I said. I was beginning to see a pattern here. "Your wish is my command," I muttered.

"That's exactly right," Jake said, his emerald eyes glinting with satisfaction as he smacked me on the rear.

***

I changed out of the paint-flecked terrycloth robe and put on the first dress I grabbed out of the dozens in my closet. I felt a bit bad that I'd already ruined two of his robes with paint. I told myself that I'd keep this one for painting.

Look at me. Making myself feel at home.

I shrugged off the faint feeling of jealousy and longing. This was my home for the week, at least, and I should enjoy it while I had the chance to. When I came out of the bedroom to the kitchen, Jake was putting away his cell phone. He whistled a low whistle when he saw me, then lifted his phone in the air.

"I thought that we could order in," Jake said, waving the phone in his hand. "So that you don't die of starvation in the middle of New York City. How does that sound?"

"Sure," I said. "What do you feel like?"

"Sushi. I already ordered."

"Well, thanks for making all of my decisions so easy," I said.

"Did you want something else?" Jake asked, one eyebrow raised.

"Sushi is good."

My stomach growled with the force of a thousand lions.

"And anyway," I said, looking down at my tummy. "I definitely should have eaten lunch. Although I don't know, maybe this is a good way for me to diet."

"What, getting so engrossed in your painting that you forget to eat lunch?"

"I'll call it the Artist's Diet," I said. "I'll make millions off of the website with affiliate sales. *Paint the pounds away.*"

Jake laughed.

"Don't get too skinny," he said, coming around to place his palms on my hips. He caressed me gently and his voice growled in my ear. "I like *this* too much."

The doorbell rang, and I started back, stepping on Jake's feet. I jumped off immediately and bumped my hip against the table.

"Ow," I said.

"That must be the chef," Jake said.

"The *chef?*"

Jake returned with a Japanese man in a chef's hat and apron following him. The chef had a black suitcase in tow. I watched as he placed the suitcase on the kitchen counter and opened it up. A row of gleaming silver knifes unrolled from one side, and in the other was an ice-packed array of…

"Is that fish?" I asked, leaning closer. Jake sat on one of the kitchen stools next to me. From here we could see everything the chef did.

"Fresh," the sushi chef said. "Caught this morning. You like tuna?"

"I love tuna."

"Good."

The chef made his way around the kitchen like it was his own, and I realized that this must not be the first time he'd come here. Jake poured out three glasses of something clear and steaming from a ceramic carafe. He pushed one of the glasses to me and another to the chef, who was busy setting up a pot full of rice to boil.

"Cheers," he said, lifting his glass. The chef held his glass up in appreciation and drank. I did the same. Then I bent over, coughing.

"Oh my God!" I cried. The drink had seared my throat, but not because of the heat. I felt the alcohol hit my system after the first sip. "What is this?"

"Sake," Jake said, smiling at me. "Have you never had any?"

"Wow," I said. "Not like this."

"Very good," the chef said, smiling broadly as he emptied his glass. Jake poured him another.

"It's...uh... interesting," I said. Not bad, but I would stick to rum and cokes in the future. This stuff was *strong*.

The chef quickly sliced up paper-thin strips of ginger into a small bowl and plated it next to some wasabi. With his knife, he sliced into the thick cut of tuna.

It was incredible to watch. The chef's knife was as quick and precise as a surgeon's, and he deftly sliced up a plate of tuna, serving it with the ginger and wasabi.

"Sashimi," he said brusquely, and stirred the rice.

I sipped my sake and mimicked Jake as he picked up a piece of fish with his fingers and ate.

"This is delicious," I said, my mouth around the sashimi. The fatty cut of tuna tasted like butter melting onto my tongue. It was light and fresh and perfect.

The chef kept working, and once he saw that I was interested, he began to narrate his steps to Jake and me.

"This is nori," he said, holding out a dark green sheet.

"Oh man, I always just referred to it as *that seaweed stuff*," I said. "Sorry. We don't get much sushi in Iowa."

The chef placed the seaweed sheet—sorry, the *nori* sheet—on top of a bamboo mat. He dipped his hands under the faucet.

"Cold water," he explained. "It makes it easier to handle the rice."

"Hmm," I said, scrutinizing the way his hands moved as he worked. He spread the rice over the nori sheet, leaving part of the last edge uncovered. Then he took a large strip of tuna and laid it across the whole sheet.

"Some fresh cucumber as well," he said. His chef's knife moved like lightning over the cucumber, cutting it into nearly transparent tiny strips.

"Then," he said, his fingers rolling the mat away from him, "you roll it up."

He pressed down on top of the rolled up mat and then unrolled it. With his knife, he cut up the sushi roll like it was a carrot, producing a half dozen perfect pieces of sushi which he plated with two swoops of his knife.

"See?" he said. "Easy as pie."

"Holy cow," I cried. "That's incredible! It looks like a piece of art." The rolls were pink and white and green arced over the plate, and he garnished it with a few green sprigs and some pink fish eggs to top it off.

"Lacey, would you like to start a career as a sushi chef?" Jake teased.

"I'll stick to making *art* art. I'm much better at eating sushi art," I teased back, and reached for a roll.

Chapter Six

After dinner, Jake held out his hand.

"Where are we going?" I asked innocently.

"You know exactly where we're going," he said.

At once a flare of heat streaked through my body. The soft curve at the corner of his mouth made me ache to kiss him. But how could I, if that wasn't what he wanted?

His fingers clasped mine and I followed obediently as he led me down the hallway. I was wearing a dress—one of his dresses, but I was barefoot, and the carpet rose between my toes as I walked next to him.

"You've been such a good girl, Lacey," he said. "I'm going to give you a little reward. Would you like that?"

He opened the door to the room I'd woken up in. I walked in. After having been here before, it seemed strangely familiar. The mirror taking up the whole wall behind the bed. The chains leading from the bedposts. The art—

"Is this Kage?" I asked. I'd seen lettering on the side of one of the walls that I hadn't noticed before. It reminded me of the painting in his art gallery, the one by the famous street artist. I stepped closer to the wall, drifting my fingers along the lines. "It looks like his stuff. Did you get him to come—"

"On the bed," Jake ordered.

I turned around.

"Oh, so you can't answer a simple question."

"There are no questions in here," he said blankly. "And you'll be spanked for that one."

"Really?" I said, pulling away from the wall. A thrill ran through me at the memory of his hand coming down on my ass.

"That's another question," Jake warned.

"Well, if I'm already going to be spanked, I might as well ask—"

Jake was across the room in a split second. He yanked me by the arm, sat on the bed, and pulled me off of my feet. All of a sudden I was bending over his lap. My feet scrabbled for purchase, but he had me completely off-balance.

"Ahh!" I cried. "I'm sorry, okay? Okay?"

He didn't listen. Or if he did listen, he didn't care. In the mirror I saw him pull up the hem of my dress roughly, exposing my bare ass. He raised his hand and then I didn't see anything more. My eyes were closed.

His hand came down with a hard clap on my ass. I squealed, writhing involuntarily with the pain of the blow. Then again, again.

I grabbed with my hands but there was nothing to grab, nothing except his leg. I held on for dear life as his hand came down, sending sharp echoes through the room that bounced off of the mirror and came back to my ears in reverberations that thrilled me almost as much as the real thing. The sound filled my ears, and I moaned along with it.

After only a minute of spanking, a minute that felt like an hour, I became aware of a threading feeling between my thighs. He would spank me hard, then run his fingers between my legs, grazing my slit.

I was already wet. I didn't know when it had happened, but his fingers sliding over me spread my moisture over my folds, over my clit that was already pulsing with desire.

God, he could make me aroused so quickly. I didn't know how, but the pain of the spanks sent equal shudders of pleasure through me, building the pressure inside. With every clap against my skin, explosions of red burst behind my eyelids and I cried out. I didn't know if I was crying for him to stop or crying for him to spank me harder. By this point, I didn't care.

His hand slid roughly between my thighs, kneading me with an ungentle touch. I squealed and grabbed again, tearing at the bedsheet hanging off of the side of the bed.

Jake tossed me onto the bed. I rolled out of his arms and landed on my hands and feet on the mattress. I was astonished at how strong he was, that he could pick me up like I was nothing. He stripped off his jacket and threw it onto the floor, then began to unbutton his shirt.

I squealed and tried to crawl away, but he was too fast. He grabbed my ankles with his hands and flipped me over bodily. I landed on the soft bed and clutched at the sheet as he dragged me to the edge.

"You're making this terribly difficult," he said. Without another word he plunged his tongue deep into me, his hands wrenching my thighs apart. I squealed as he thrust his tongue into me, bursts of pleasure exploding along my nerves. I couldn't stop myself from raising my hips to meet him.

He sucked hard at my clit, then pulled away just as I was reaching release. His lips slid along my folds. Then sucked hard, then pulled away. It was impossible for me to know what was coming next, only that when I was on the edge of reaching pleasure, he didn't give it to me.

I moaned and arched against the bed, needing him utterly.

"Please," I moaned. "Please take me. Please—"

He jerked back his head and I cried out with need. I was hollow inside, desperately wanting him to fill me.

Instead, he grabbed my wrist and pulled me up, locking the handcuff around my wrist as he did so.

"Jake—"

I'd said his name before, but this time his eyes flashed with pain and I felt his hurt as though it were my own. How could a single word have so much power over him?

He said nothing as he grabbed my other hand and pulled it out, locking it in place. His hand pulled the chains, and I was jerked upright to my knees, my arms stretched out to the sides and slightly upward.

"Please, I won't say it again," I said. "I promise, I swear. I'll swear on anything I won't."

I was babbling, needing to say anything to fill the silence. He couldn't leave me like this, unfinished. He couldn't. And yet, when he turned away, my words trailed off to nothing. I could see his hurt and it shamed me.

My heart sank as he turned away from me to the mirror. He looked up, and although his eyes saw me, they weren't seeing me, and I wasn't seeing him. Not really. We were both just reflections.

I panted, catching my breath, unwilling to move my gaze from his. I wanted him so badly, but I wanted more. I wanted to know why he was like this. I wanted to know him.

The real him.

Chapter Seven

"I'm sorry," he said. His green eyes burned in the reflection of the dim light. His arms were tense at his sides, the muscles drawn tight against his skin.

"Sorry for what?" I asked.

"I can't... I don't know how to explain."

He stared at the mirror. He wasn't looking at me anymore. He was looking ahead into his own reflection with an accusatory stare.

"Does this have to do with your family?" I asked softly. I wanted to know. I needed to know. And at the same time, I was scared to ask. Scared that he might not let me into his private life.

Scared that he would.

"What do you know about them?"

I shook my head slightly.

"Nothing. Lucas mentioned it. When we were at the restaurant. He said I should ask you about it."

A long, dreadful pause followed.

"My family is dead," he said.

"Dead?" I echoed the word in surprise. That was one thing I hadn't expected. Maybe it was that I couldn't imagine my own family dead, my mother and father, my brothers. To hear him say it so calmly made the thought even more frightening.

"It was a long time ago. I was a child."

I waited for him to continue. He stared into the mirror, not looking at me, only looking at his own face. His expression turned to hatred.

"My name is Jake Carville Jr. My full name. Did you know that?"

I shook my head.

"No. After your dad?"

He nodded.

"My dad was the one who left me this fortune. He was a rich, abusive drunk who hated his employees. But he hated me more."

"Why?"

"I didn't want to continue his business. He worked as an insurance executive. Do you know how bad it was? All he talked about was his work. About how much money he could scrape out of people. How he could scare people into buying insurance they didn't need. Life insurance, car insurance, home insurance. He trained his salesmen to bully and threaten customers until they bought more, more, more."

He paused for a moment, his face turning red. He breathed slowly. He was standing so still that I almost couldn't see his chest rising and falling.

"He beat me," Jake said, and although his voice stayed calm I saw the corner of his eye twitch when he said it. "He beat me, and if he had enough to drink he'd beat my mom, too. One time my little brother was crying and he screamed at her to make it stop. She tried to shush him, but nothing worked, not even his pacifier. I remember he started to shake the baby—"

His voice broke, and I longed to go to him. Tears stung my eyes. I wanted to put my arms around him, to hold him, to tell him that it was alright. But I was tied to the bed and I couldn't. Maybe he had planned it that way.

"She grabbed his arm to try to stop him and he swung at her. Not with his hand, either, but with a fist."

Jake's eyes glazed over. He was lost in his own world of memories. I didn't say anything. I didn't want him to stop, although it hurt me to hear his pain. My chest clenched as he continued.

"And her nose broke with this awful crack—I remember thinking I had never seen so much blood before. She was screaming and he just kept hitting her and hitting her, and she had her arms around the baby and she was bleeding all over him."

He released a shaky sigh.

"Afterwards he had his private doctor come and stitch her up. The doctor didn't say anything. My father paid him well enough that he didn't say anything. My mom lay in bed and cried. And I cleaned up my brother in the sink. I washed all of her blood off of him."

Now I was crying, trying not to sob aloud, and tears rolled down my cheeks. Still, I listened to him remember his family.

"I'm telling you this so that you'll understand… what I did. Or what I didn't do, I guess. So that you'll know why it happened the way it did."

I waited, unable to wipe the tears from my cheeks.

"One night, after my mom had put me to bed, I snuck out to go get a late night snack. My dad had drunk enough that he'd passed out in his office. I don't remember why, but I went by the hallway and saw smoke coming from under the door."

"It was stupid, maybe, but I was curious. I was always a curious little kid. And I pushed the door open."

Jake's voice grew rasping. Like he was crying, but without the tears.

"And the whole room was on fire. He had passed out on his desk, and I could see the papers burning from his cigar, and the carpet had caught fire behind him where one of the papers had blown off. There was smoke everywhere."

He bent his head down suddenly, shaking it from side to side. For a long minute he said nothing.

"What happened?"

It was the first question I'd asked. I wasn't supposed to ask questions. But he turned and looked at me, and his eyes were hollow with pain, so hurt that he didn't even care.

"I didn't save him," Jake said.

"Your dad?"

"No. My brother. I— I ran to my mother's room but she wasn't there, and I didn't see my brother anywhere. I thought I heard her voice calling but I must have imagined it because I didn't see her anywhere. I'd left the door to his office open and the smoke was billowing out of the door too fast and I couldn't see anything. So I ran away. I ran down the stairs and let him die. I let them all die."

My mouth dropped open. Jake looked up at me, and there were no tears on his face but his eyes were burning with hurt.

He turned back to the mirror and looked at himself, but I knew that he was looking at his dad.

"The firefighters found me in the stairwell, huddled in the corner. All I could say was that it was my fault, *my fault.* They took me away and put out the fire, but everything had burned to ash. My family. Everything."

I swallowed the lump in my throat.

"How old were you?"

"Four and a half."

My face contorted in grief. Imagining Jake as a little boy running through the fire and smoke, finally fleeing... I couldn't get the image out of my mind.

He breathed in and out again, the vapor of his breath misting the mirror.

"It was my fault they died," he said. "I tried to save them but I couldn't find her quick enough. I couldn't see—"

"It wasn't your fault," I said.

Suddenly he slammed his fist into the mirror. It cracked into a spiderweb of fractures where his hand had hit it.

"They're dead!" he yelled. His voice filled the room and when he turned on me there was a fury in his eyes that chilled me to the core. "Dead!"

My breaths hitched but I didn't say anything. There wasn't anything I could say.

Chapter Eight

For the next few days, Jake didn't speak to me again about his family, and I didn't bring it up.

He left me during the days to paint, and tied me up at night in the mirrored room. When he tied me up, I remembered not to call him Jake. His father's name.

He never took my virginity, but oh! The other things he did to me scorched my body and sent me into gasping orgasms.

The first night after he told me his story, he bound me not with handcuffs, but with a long silk tie that he wound around my entire body. I was immobilized on the bed, and he rolled me over, sinking his tongue deep into me until I shuddered and shook, my thighs clenched around his head.

The second night he tied me down on my back. I didn't know what he was going to do until the first drips of red candlewax fell onto my chest. I screamed. I writhed. The pain was almost too much, but somehow it went right around and soon I was screaming with pleasure as the red hot wax ran down my thighs.

My screams had been too much for Jake, too. I'd barely managed to catch my breath when he pulled his cock out of his pants. He didn't even need to stroke it, just gripped it hard at the base as he came all over my chest. His white cum shot out and dripped over my skin, mixing with the red wax as he panted, leaning over me. I swore he was going to kiss me then, but he didn't.

He never once kissed me on the mouth.

***

I thought that had been the worst of it. That somehow I'd exhausted his imagination of painful pleasures.

How wrong. How utterly wrong.

The next time he tied me up, it was upright. My arms held me swinging and my toes barely touched the sheets. I was hanging like a fly caught in a spiderweb. And Jake was the spider.

When he brought out the crop I almost fainted. Not that it would have mattered much, I suppose. He would have slapped me to bring me around. But I couldn't stop staring at what he held in his hand.

A thin leather strap at the end of a knotted rod. It probably shouldn't have looked so scary, but after having my skin spanked pink I was ready to run.

Jake trailed the crop down along my side down to my hip. The leather felt cool, almost welcome against the burning of my skin, but I knew what he was going to do with it.

At least, I thought I did.

At first, it was light whips across my asscheeks. I yelped through the gag he'd casually knotted around my mouth. Stripes of pain made me twist like a helpless animal of prey. Yes, prey. Jake was a predator, and he didn't bother to hide it. When he went around behind me, I sobbed in terror and anticipation.

Despite it all, I wanted him. I wanted the predator to catch me. I needed him to tear me apart and put me back together. I thrilled under his touch, no matter how harsh. But I had never thought that he would do this to me.

The crop whipped me again, but this time it was against my already-slick folds. I screamed. Oh God, I screamed. The ache of wanting him was too much combined with the burning whip of the riding crop between my thighs.

Again, he struck me. Again. Again. And he continued to whip me until the pain turned to pleasure and I came, the orgasm jerking me into unconsciousness.

When I woke, his cock was sliding between my asscheeks. I moaned, feeling his thick shaft press through between my thighs, then back.

Was this it? Would he finally take me?

I had spent the past few days in terrible anticipation of this moment, but now that it was here all I could do was choke out a groan of need. The tip of his cock pressed against my entrance, and then—

And then—

He pulled back without entering me, and I sobbed as he came, the thick ropes of white dripping down my ass and between my thighs. He didn't need me like I needed him. He didn't need me at all. When he untied me, I crumpled to the bed and curled up, and he left me in the darkness.

I was his gift, to use as he pleased. But despite my longing, he would not take me.

Chapter Nine

It was the day before the end of the week. I was his gift for another twenty-four hours, and that would be all.

As usual—strange, how quickly things can become *usual*—he got ready to leave in the morning.

"Paint," he said. "I left you a gift in the studio."

With that, he was gone.

When I walked into the art studio, a terrycloth robe draped around my naked shoulders, I gaped at what I saw. A huge canvas, fifteen feet on all sides, lay flat on the floor. I'd filled up most of the smaller canvases in the room, and what had been a room of total white was now cluttered with my pieces. But this canvas was perfectly untouched, and so large that for a moment my mind dizzied with the possibilities.

"Think," I murmured to myself. "Think."

My hands gathered their materials as I thought. There had been a painting I wanted to try for a long time. In my mind, it was two forms that looked like trees, growing together intertwined. I didn't know if this was the right canvas to try it on, and I didn't know if I could pull it off, but I could try, couldn't I?

As I painted, my frustrations grew. The painting was so big that I couldn't get a good look at the whole of it, and I was relegated to painting it in parts, bit by bit.

Lunch came and went. Jake had taken to having one of his servants stop by to drop off a sandwich at the door of the art studio, but when they knocked this time I shouted for them to leave me alone. Stupid food. Stupid art. I wasn't hungry. I could eat after I'd finished.

I used rollers to put in the background colors, but when I stepped back I frowned in dismay.

No. Not quite like that. The light wasn't right. Everything was the same value, nothing stood out.

I backed away from the huge canvas and tried on a smaller one, a rectangle. I sketched out the crude lines of what I had in mind, then blocked in the colors. It took me about an hour to get the shapes the way I wanted them. I squinted at the smaller piece. It looked alright, but the large canvas was square, and I didn't know quite how to crop it down.

"Square canvases," I said, riffling through the canvases I had left. None of them were perfect squares— I'd used up all of those. I looked at the pieces I'd already done, but it hurt me to think about painting over them.

Then I looked over at the black door.

Storage, he'd said. What if there was a square canvas in there I could use?

No. He'd specifically told me not to go in there. I shook my head and turned back to the painting. I tried a different shade of blue for the background, something a little lighter.

It took a while just to cover up the parts I'd already painted, stepping carefully around the parts that weren't dry. Finally I put the last block of color in and set my brush aside. I went to the bottom of the canvas and stared at the damned thing.

"ARGH!"

It was wrong, all wrong. Jake had given me this gift, and I'd wasted it. The afternoon was almost over, and he would be back soon, and I had nothing, absolutely nothing to show for it. I sat down with a thud on the edge of the canvas, looking balefully over my paintings.

Today was the last day. Would I even get to keep these? Where would I put them, even if he did let me keep them?

Useless, completely useless. And, just as quickly as I'd realized my painting was worthless, anger seized me.

"Junk!" I cried, shoving the paintings by the handful into the corners. I went through all of them, one by one. Some of them were flowers, abstract and curving. Some were names, my tag mostly, and these I threw with force against the wall.

It was all useless junk, anyway. I had no real talent. I had no eye for this. I hated that I'd wasted all of this time painting, but mostly I hated that I'd wasted all of these materials.

I slammed my hand against the wall, then kicked a canvas that had fallen over to the floor. In a fury, I went around the room, kicking aside all of the paintings that I hated so much. I went to kick one in front of the storage door and stubbed my toe against the door. A shooting pain stabbed through my foot.

"Shit!" I screamed, not even caring that I was swearing. And then I was slamming my hand against the black storage door, screaming every curse word I'd bottled in for the past nineteen years. I screamed them all, and made up some new ones, and it was only when I heard a clatter of metal that I stopped.

The padlock had broken off to the side. It dangled uselessly on a hinge. God, had I hit the door hard enough to break it? For a split second, I thought idiotically that Jake would make me pay to fix it.

Then I noticed something through the crack in the door, and forgot everything else.

***

My anger gave way to curiosity as I slowly pushed the storage door open. I flipped on the light and a bulb above clicked on, shining brightly into the forbidden room.

It was a storage room, alright, but nearly as large as the one that I was in. And it was filled top to bottom with canvases.

Only these canvases weren't white. Someone had used them already. I stepped gingerly past the door and looked at the paintings. Jake must keep all of the art here, I thought, all of the paintings he'd bought that weren't currently on display. I could see a few more Kage paintings, as well as some charcoal sketches that were unsigned.

Crazy. This room alone must house a million dollars of art.

Carefully, I pulled some of the canvases away from the walls to flip through them. A charcoal sketch with lettering. Another pastel. And underneath—

I frowned, pulling the back canvas out. It was a painting by Kage, that was for sure. It was his lettering, his broad sweeps and bright colors. But it wasn't finished. The painting ended halfway down the canvas, with the rest of the lettering only partially filled in with pencil sketches.

I'd never seen a half-finished painting by Kage before. I held it up to the light to see it better, and—

"LACEY!"

I yelped and dropped the painting. It landed with a hard crack on its corner. I jumped back, away from the door, and spun around.

Jake was standing in the doorway, anger burning his face.

"What are you doing here?" he hissed.

I bent down and picked up the Kage painting. It didn't look like the framing had cracked, but I held it carefully just in case.

"I—I—"

"Give me that!"

I held out the painting and Jake ripped it from my hands.

"I'm sorry," I said. "I only wanted—"

"Get out!"

He held the door open, and I cast one look back longingly. It was then that I realized something strange.

There were other unfinished paintings, stacked on top of each other. But all of them—

"These are all by Kage," I whispered. I stopped in my tracks.

"Lacey, I'm warning you—"

233

All of them. All of them had Kage's lettering or Kage's style.

"What are all of these?" I asked. "Why do you have so many—"

I looked back at Jake, at the way he was holding the canvas so possessively in his hands. And then I knew. Reflected in his eyes was my recognition, and his fingers turned white as they clutched the painting.

"It's you," I said, with an inward gasp.

"You're him. You're... you're Kage."

Chapter Ten

"I told you not to come into this room," Jake said.

"You're him," I repeated. "Kage. Wow. I can't believe it. I should have figured it out, but—"

"Get out!"

Jake grabbed me suddenly by the arm, tearing me out of the art storage room. I stumbled back, stepping onto the large square of canvas I'd been working on. It was forgotten now with this new revelation, and I stared at Jake like I expected paint to come gushing out of his ears.

"So is this your art studio—" I started to ask, but the look on Jake's face stopped me cold. He was mad. And not just upset. His eyes burned with fury. He tossed the painting back behind him into the storage area and slammed the door.

"You," he spat. He took a step toward me. I retreated, and my foot caught on the canvas. I fell backwards and landed with a hard thunk on top of my painting. My hands slipped in the wet paint as I scrabbled back away from him.

"Jake—I mean, Kage—I mean—"

Jake took one step toward me and I shut my mouth. His shoes squelched against the paint, leaving footprints in the painting.

"I'm sorry," I said quickly. "I didn't mean to. Well, I did, but only once the door was open. I…" My voice trailed off as I watched Jake's face contort with barely suppressed rage.

"You disobeyed me. After I had to spend all my willpower controlling myself around you…"

He took his jacket off and threw it to the floor.

"After I promised myself I wouldn't spoil your innocence..."

His fingers unbuttoned his shirt. I swallowed, watching him, no longer wanting to speak. I couldn't defend myself. He was right. I was in the wrong. And yet, as he spoke, I found myself hoping that somehow this— this act of unwitting defiance—had broken down the wall that kept him away from me.

"After I tried to stop myself from wanting to take you..."

"Take me!" I cried.

It was all I got out, and then Jake was on his knees, dragging me over his lap. His hands yanked the fabric of my terrycloth robe up, and then he was spanking my bare ass so hard that the blows made my body jerk with the shock of his force. I squealed as he spanked me, aware that I was instantly aroused, my body aching for his touch no matter how hard.

"Temptation!" he growled.

I shrieked as he turned me over and pinned me back, his hands pressing against my shoulders.

"I wanted so badly to keep you pure," he whispered. "You have no idea how hard it was… you have no idea how much I wanted to take you."

His face was inches from mine, and I saw my chance.

I took it.

Arching my back, I strained upward and pressed a kiss against his lips. Just one, but that was all it took.

His face contorted, the anger falling away and being replaced by confusion.

"Lacey?" he asked, gazing straight into my eyes.

"Kage," I said, calling him by the name he'd chosen for himself. My own voice seemed unfamiliar to me, older somehow. "I want you to take me."

***

"Lacey," he whispered, and then the pressure from my shoulders lifted.

I raised my head. Jake tore off his shirt, unbuckled his belt. His fingers were fast, but mine were faster as we both fumbled to unzip his pants. He got them half undone before he pulled me in close, tearing off my terrycloth robe.

Then his mouth was on mine again, and his hands were threading through my hair as he possessed me with his kiss.

Yes, possessed. That is the only word to describe it. His lips sought mine out hungrily, sucking hard and biting. I let my lips part and his tongue thrust into mine, and a blinding pressure made me arch into him. His fingers sent thrills through my scalp and all I could feel was heat, the heat scorching between my legs and the heat of his lips burning mine.

I was his, and he took my breath away as he kissed me and kissed me again. We fell back together against the wet canvas and then his hands were moving down and he was kissing my neck and shoulders, returning after each kiss to take my lips again with his. Kissing me like he forgot how to stop, like he never wanted the kiss to end.

Despite being a virgin, I'd been kissed before. This, though was something that seemed utterly different. I realized that this kiss was a prelude to something else, something more, and the thought of it shivered every part of me. I moaned into his kiss and he moaned back, pressing hard and soft alternately until I couldn't breathe. I was only gasping for air to keep myself alive but I needed his kiss more than I needed air, more than I'd ever needed anything.

His hands ran down my quivering body, searching me out. He touched me everywhere, squeezing, kneading, caressing. I gasped as his hand slipped under my ass cheeks and pulled my hips up against him. I could feel his cock erect already, straining against the fabric of his underwear.

God, I needed him. My hands were covered in paint, but I didn't care. I grabbed him, needing more, needing him right then.

I had waited all week, and I could not wait a second longer.

"Lacey," he growled. "Lacey, I can't. I can't."

"I want you," I said.

It was enough. He groaned as I pressed another kiss against him, rolling onto my side.

He shoved down his pants, exposing his cock. It was stiff and throbbing, and I slid my fingers alongside the shaft in wonder.

"Jesus, Lacey," he said.

Then his mouth seized mine again, and I was kissing him back, wanting him, wanting nothing more than for him to take me right then and there.

He rolled over so that he was on top of me. One of his hands clasped my cheek, and his thumb brushed along under my eye alongside my cheekbone. I could feel his cock pressing against my entrance. I was hot, oh so hot. He had me pinned and no matter how I squirmed I couldn't move.

"Are you sure?" He whispered the words frantically, his hand caressing my cheek with such urgency that my mouth went dry. "I don't know if I can stop myself but please, Lacey, Lacey, are you sure?"

I could not think, only feel, and my body was hollow for him. In that second, I would have done anything to make him take me. But it only took one word, and I gave it willingly.

"Yes."

He plunged into me with one thrust, and my scream of pleasure was muffled by his mouth kissing me as my body clenched itself around him.

It was a feeling such as I'd never felt before. His thickness filled me, stretched me, expanded me. There was pain, but it did not hold a candle to the pain he'd given me all week, and the pleasure–

Oh God, the pleasure. It was as though every nerve ending of mine had been set on fire. My body arched back against the canvas, and my hands pressed against his chest. He thrust again hard, further yet, impossibly deep into me. My legs wrapped around him and I could not help the small cries of pleasure as I pushed him even farther into me.

Something inside me broke open, inviting him in, and his movements made me cry out.

"Kage," I moaned.

He rolled his hips, and my orgasm swept through me like an instant fire. My head ripped from side to side as the intense waves of ecstasy came crashing down and through me. This was different from anything I had felt before, but more than that, it was different than anything I'd ever even *imagined*.

With him inside me, I felt complete somehow. Whole. It was as though I had never been satisfied before, and nothing could ever satisfy me again. Nothing except *this*.

He held me in his arms, waiting until the waves of my orgasm had subsided. I was breathless, gasping ragged breaths from the air.

"Oh, my beautiful. My Lacey," he said. He pressed a tender kiss to me. That was the last tender motion, and then I shifted beneath him and his eyes turned wild.

Jake rolled into me again and did not stop, his body shuddering mine with his thrusts. The rhythm grew faster and faster as he thrust into me again and again. I could feel the pressure inside me building even then, even as the thrills of my last orgasm were waning.

My hands scrambled at the canvas underneath me, but the paint there was wet and there was nothing to hold on to. I gripped Jake's shoulders and twined my legs around him to try and hold on as tightly as I could.

Moaning, I matched his rhythm, rocking my hips up to meet him.

"Oh Jesus, Lacey," he said. His hair hung over his face. I put one hand to his cheek. His skin was hot, moist with sweat. His eyes drilled holes into me.

"Harder," I whispered.

Before the word was out of my mouth, he'd gripped me into his strong arms and thrust again. I screamed as he jackhammered his cock into me, slamming into my flesh over and over again. My nerves were exploding with pleasure and I held onto him, my body clenching tight around his shaft. He was hard as rock. His body crashed into mine, unraveling any last resistance I might have had.

My body was uncontrollable now, my hair tossing in the wet paint, my hands scratching at his back. He thrust into me over and over again in a raw, primal rhythm that sent me higher, higher, until I was standing at the precipice looking over into the abyss. I closed my eyes and saw stars.

Then he took me over the edge, fucking me hard and raw, fucking me with wild abandon. Rutting like animals, we rolled over each other, clawing at skin. He kissed me and the kiss turned into a bite, and then his teeth were on my shoulder and I was spasming in his arms.

There was nothing left of me, Lacey. There was nothing left of the girl who had walked into this place. There was only need, a sharp hot need, and as my orgasm ripped through me I disappeared and all that was left was pure sensation, hands and mouths and the waves of pleasure coursing through my body.

Another spasm went through my body and then I felt him jerk once and still over me. He moaned, a thick noise in his throat, and his hot seed spilled inside of me. I pulled his mouth to mine and shuddered once more with him as we spent our last climax together.

Chapter Eleven

I lay my head back against the hard canvas, gasping for air. After the orgasm's last throes had faded, Jake rolled to his side. I let out a soft sigh as he withdrew, his cock sliding slowly out of me. My body grasped for him, clenching, and then relaxed.

He clasped me to his side, and in his arms I breathed easily. He held me as though I was some delicate, fragile thing, cradling me softly. There was no hint of the man who had thrust hard and fast into my body, no whisper of the man who had bit down on my shoulder as he came, groaning and hard, into my core.

There was only *him*.

As I breathed in deeply, my chest rose and fell. I felt myself relaxing. A week of sleeping as long as I wanted to, a week of painting my heart's desire—and now this.

He'd taken me in completely, *taken* me completely. But it was only now that I felt his outer walls crumbling down, letting me into his private world.

"Lacey," he said. His thumb tilted my chin up, and I looked into his deeply concerned eyes.

"What is it?" I asked.

"Are you alright?"

I burst out laughing, and if he hadn't been holding me so tightly I would have rolled over the floor in laughter. He looked at me curiously until I had stopped. I wiped a tear of laughter from my eyes.

"Seriously? You kidnapped me, blindfolded me… you've been using hot wax and chains and whips on me, and *now* is the first time you think to ask me if I'm alright?"

"Well, I—"

"I'm fine. That's your answer. No, I'm more than fine. I'm thrilled."

"Thrilled?"

"Yes, that's the word," I said, placing both of my hands on his broad chest. "You thrill me in every way. It started with the elevator."

"The elevator?"

I nodded primly.

"I was scared to death of that thing. It made my stomach do somersaults. And then your art collection—"

"You can't be thrilled by a bunch of paintings."

"I can and I am. And they're *yours*." I poked him in the chest, remembering the revelation that had led to all of this.

"Mine?"

"You are Kage. *You!* How could you not tell me? How could you not let me know?"

"Nobody knows."

"Nobody?"

Jake's brows knitted together.

"Lacey, you're the only one who's ever even come close to guessing. Except the police commissioner, of course. He's the one I had to bribe to get out of jail the one time I got caught."

"How'd you get caught?" I asked.

"Oh," Jake said, slumping his head back and smiling at the ceiling. "It's stupid. I was so stupid."

"Tell me. It'll help me get over my inferiority complex."

"If anybody shouldn't have a complex—"

"While lying next to a handsome multitalented billionaire."

"Multitalented?"

"Your art. And your tongue. Two excellent talents."

"I'm glad that I have you to practice my talents on," he said. "And I was caught in an alley behind one of my own buildings. Of course, I had to pretend that it wasn't *my* building, because the cops who caught me would never have believed me. I was putting up a piece next to one of those *COPS* tags. Have you seen them?"

"Yeah, the ones with the donut for the *O*? I see those everywhere."

"And they thought I was the one who'd done it. Never mind that my painting was right there, obviously wet. So they put cuffs on me and took me in."

"You criminal," I teased.

"Well, I didn't have any ID on me. I was dressed for it, you know, hoodie and ripped jeans. Nobody knew who I was at the police station. But I'd had dinner with the commissioner just the week before. Oh, man, the look on his face when he came in and saw me in a jail cell!"

"Lucky for you," I said.

"There's no luck to any of it," Jake sighed, his eyes turning dark. "If I was a poor kid, I'd still be in jail. This city runs on money, as stupid as that is."

"Well, I'm glad you're out of jail," I said. "Although I think I'd like to see you in cuffs sometime."

"You'll have to put me in them first," he said, a smile breaking across his face.

"I'll take that as a challenge."

He stood up and lifted me off of the floor. His head tilted at the canvas, and when I saw what he was looking at, I could have died.

Where we had been lying down, there was a splotch of my blood. I looked down and saw a smear on the inside of my thigh.

"I didn't even feel it," I whispered. "I mean, I felt it, but it wasn't... there wasn't much pain at all."

"Take a break from art," he said. "Take a bath. Go read for a while. Eat something."

"Sure," I said. My face burned red. I turned quickly away from the canvas.

"I have some more work to do," Jake said. "I want you dressed and ready to go out by eight tonight."

"I'm going to need something to wear other than dresses."

"Not tonight. Not where I'm taking you."

I put my hands on my hip and stared after him as he strolled down the hallway.

"Oh?" I asked. Despite trying to sound vexed, I was sure he could hear the thrill of anticipation in my voice. "And where are you taking me?"

"Somewhere *awesome,*" he said.

"Awesome?"

"Awesome," he repeated.

"Awesome," I said, and sighed as he walked away from me.

***

I actually spent quite a bit of time getting ready. After my bath, I picked out a dark red dress that hung sleek and silken over my curves. The top was a bit low, but I thought it would be nice to give Jake what he wanted.

I spent a half hour in the mirror, trying on different shades of eye shadow. I settled on a smoky gray, like the kind Steph had put on me that first night.

It had been a week. The days had passed by quickly, but I felt, strangely enough, that I'd been living here forever. The rooms had become familiar. And most of my hours had been spent in total focus, painting in the studio by myself.

As I stood up and examined my dress for any lumps or bumps, I could hardly recognize myself. This wasn't the Lacey who had strolled through here with a cake in her arms. I felt taller, more confident. I felt...

I felt beautiful.

Jake's mouth dropped open when I walked into the living room.

"My God, Lacey," he said, standing up to greet me. I felt so elegant as he bent his head to kiss me lightly on the lips.

"You like?"

"I—wow. Yes. Very much." Jake was stammering, and it was cute to see him look so astonished. Maybe I would have to wear dresses more often.

"Where are we going?" I asked.

"It's a secret," Jake said.

"Right. Somewhere awesome."

"Come on," he said, taking my elbow. "I can't wait. You're going to stop everybody in their tracks."

"Stop who?" I asked, but he only led me to the elevator, winking in secrecy.

There was no limo downstairs.

"We're not going far," said Jake, but he didn't tell me where.

We walked down the street slowly. I rested my hand on Jake's arm, but the heels didn't bother me all that much. Not now that I was walking by his side. As we walked, heads turned to stare at us, both men and women.

I felt so confident with Jake by my side. As we turned the corner, I realized that we were on the street of art galleries. This was where I hung out on my days off, pretending that I had enough money to buy any of the painting that hung inside.

"Do you see it?" he said, stopping in front of a gallery window.

I looked inside and my heart skipped a beat.

"Oh my. Oh my," I repeated. I didn't know what else to say. "Oh. My."

It was my painting. My paintings. A whole wall of them. The sign in front of the shop said *Show Opening.*

"No," I said, gripping Jake's hand with all my strength. "It's not—"

"It's your show."

My lips trembled. My own gallery show? I shook my head.

"You didn't... you did this?"

"I did this," Jake admitted, laughing slightly at my reaction. "I put some of Kage's stuff in there as well, just so you know. A week of your stuff will almost fill a gallery, but not quite."

I saw one of the Kage paintings hanging inside on a wall, right next to mine. I swallowed hard. To have my stuff on display here—next to Kage—was just incredible. As much as I tried, I couldn't let it sink in.

"Come on. Let's go inside." Jake tugged at my hand.

The attendant inside the door handed us glasses of wine and plates of cheese. I ate and drank as Jake led me around the gallery, but I couldn't taste a thing. All I could do was stare at the paintings—

My paintings—

He had taken my paintings and put them in a gallery. And people—oh, God, people were walking around and looking at my work, talking about the pieces. Women in cocktail dresses and men in suit jackets, sipping wine and looking at my pieces like they were real art, not just something on the side of a subway car.

I swallowed hard. Conflicting feelings ran through me as I took in the people at the show. Then Jake took my arm and led me around a corner to the main gallery wall.

I stared at the wall, my mouth slowly dropping open in horror.

It was the painting we'd had sex on. There, up on display for all of New York City to see. My eyes traced the handprints, the dark red stain.

"How could you?" I asked Jake.

"How could I…" He arched his eyebrow at me. "Oh. That. I had them deliver it while you were in the tub. Just in time, too. I hadn't decided what to put up as the main exhibit."

My cheeks nearly burst with color.

249

"That's not—I didn't paint that for anyone else!"

"Oh, don't worry. That one's not for sale. It's only on exhibition."

"Only on *exhibition*?" I hissed.

"What on earth are you so upset about?" Jake asked, taking me by the arm and suavely leading me forward. "Really? I can't put it on exhibition?"

"Tell me it's not under my name."

"It's not under your name."

"Is it under yours?"

"Let's see," he said. He gestured to the wall next to the painting.

"First Love," I read. "By *Unknown*. K&L Studios."

I turned to him with a question on my face.

"Kage and Lace Studios," he said, kissing my temple. "I rather like your name."

"Are you serious?" My heart was pounding, and I couldn't understand Jake's satisfied expression. I felt like everybody in the room was looking at us, staring at me. Like they knew that I was an impostor. Like they knew that the painting I was standing under was impossibly obscene.

"I can't... why are you doing this?" I asked in a low voice.

"I thought it would make you happy?"

I wanted to scream. I wasn't his wife or his girlfriend. I was an escort, someone he'd picked out at a birthday party to keep as a playtoy. He shouldn't have done this. It was all so overwhelming, and now... to have him put up this painting for everyone to see...

I stammered as I tried to make my thoughts into words for him.

"It has! I mean, it did. I *am*. But all of this—"

I flung my hand out toward the crowd and hissed under my voice.

"This is too much for a one-week fling."

It was barely imperceptible. Something in his face hardened, clenched. Then it disappeared, and a frozen smile stayed glued to his lips for the next second before disappearing too.

"I'm sorry to surprise you with all of this. Of course I should have given you more notice."

"I only meant—"

"Come," Jake said.

He gripped my arm and pulled me through the crowd, until we reached a door in the back. He opened it and motioned for me to go inside. I went. It was the back area of the gallery.

"Why are you doing this?" I asked.

Jake spun on me, green fire dancing in his eyes.

"I'm sorry," he said bluntly. "I thought you'd be happy with this. But I've obviously made a mistake."

"That's not what I'm saying."

"Then what are you saying?" he asked.

"That I don't understand what you're doing here. Why are you doing all this for me?"

"Trust me," Jake hissed, "it was only a small gesture. Do you know how much it costs to rent out an art gallery for a month?"

"I—I don't know—"

"Neither do I." He threw up his hands. "The cost doesn't matter to me in the slightest."

"So all this. Putting together an art gallery for me. It was that easy?"

Jake's eyes were narrow slits, and my anger was bubbling forward, ready to boil out of me. Jake was looking so smug, so arrogant. So unlike how he really was.

Oh, come on, Lacey. Do you think you have the slightest clue who Jake Carville really is?

I wanted to smack my inner voice and respond with a big fat yes, but I couldn't. Not when Jake was acting like this.

"I point at things and I have them," he said. "That's how easy it is for me." He shrugged, and my head nearly popped off.

"Great," I said. "Then maybe you can point to one of the other girls out there tonight."

"Lacey, for God's sake—"

"Wouldn't want you to leave a room empty overnight. That's prime penthouse space. Wouldn't want you to have to pretend to care about your weekly escort—"

"I wasn't!" Jake yelled. I darted a glance to the door, but he grabbed my arm. My breath left my chest with a whoosh as he shoved me back against the door.

Chapter Twelve

"Ah!" I cried out. Jake's body was pressed up against mine, his hand gripping my hip.

"I wasn't pretending," he said.

"Wh-what—"

"With you. I was never pretending." Jake suddenly realized what he was doing, and he let go of me. I slumped back against the door, gasping for breath.

"I'm sorry, Lacey," he said, looking down at his hands as though they were acting of their own accord. "I'm so so sorry. I didn't mean to—"

"So you do care?"

He looked up at me then, his wounded emerald eyes seeking mine out for forgiveness. I crossed my arms. I wasn't about to give in that easily, not even if his gaze made my heart melt in my chest.

"You do care about me. Is that what you're saying?"

It took him a moment. Like a root being wrenched from the ground, his admission came struggling out of his words.

"I care more about you than anyone I've ever cared about, Lacey." He reached forward and brushed my cheek with his thumb. I trembled into his hand. "I care about you more than you know."

"Good," I stammered. "I—I care about you too."

"I know this is a bit much, but I wanted to show you how much I care." Jake rubbed the back of his neck in a gesture that was oddly vulnerable and endearing. My heart swelled.

"Thank you," I said softly. "Thank you. Really. I'm sorry I freaked out. It was just... it felt like a bit much. Especially the... uh, *our* painting. I didn't mean to make you think I don't appreciate it."

"Then this—all of this—"

"It's okay," I said, smiling weakly. "It's more than okay, actually. It's awesome."

"I really am glad you like it."

"It was very sweet of you."

"It took me a while to put together the show, but it was well worth the effort."

"Wait." I said. Shock ran through me. "Back up a second. You put together the show? As in, set up all of the paintings and decided on the layout?"

"It's one of my hobbies, setting up shows. I did a great Dali exhibit once in Barcelona."

"So you actually did everything here?" I was astonished.

"Didn't you wonder where I was going in the mornings? Or that I'd taken some of your paintings? Did you really not notice that?"

"I thought you had to do, you know, work. Businessman stuff. And they're not my paintings, I mean, you gave me the canvases and paint and everything, so technically—"

"I hate business," Jake said. "I really have no head for it."

"Shut up," I said. He couldn't be serious.

"It's true. The key is to hire assistants who run my business better than I could and pay them well."

"And what do you get a salary for?" I teased.

"For coming up with all of the good ideas. Like this."

"This gallery? You think a gallery with my art is going to be profitable?"

Jake smiled and put his arms around me. He kissed the top of my head. Immediately I felt a warmth spread through my chest. I leaned against him, hugging him tightly. He cared. He cared about me.

"I hear we've already got an offer on the next painting from *Unknown*. She's a quite renowned art collector in Manhattan. A cool hundred grand, which is more than I've ever heard for a new name in the business."

"Seriously?"

'Seriously. *Unknown* might have to make some more paintings."

"Is that so? I think I can persuade *Unknown* to get back into the studio." I thought of what we'd done to create that painting, and I flushed. Jake saw my pink cheeks and brushed them with his thumb knowingly.

"There'll never be a painting quite like that first one," Jake said, smirking.

"I'm sure we'll think of something," I said, my heart filled to bursting.

"Are you ready to go back into the crowd?" Jake asked.

I nodded. Now that I knew he cared, now that I knew he was behind me at every step, I felt like I could handle anything that the world could throw at me.

Chapter Thirteen

After the show, we headed back to the house. Jake didn't waste a moment before taking me directly to the mirrored room.

Now, as though seeing it for the first time, I walked around, looking at the art painted on the walls. There was darkness there, but a darkness that hinted at something underneath.

Something burning to get out.

"Lacey, don't make me have to spank you before you climb up on the bed." His voice smiled with a warning.

"I only wanted to see your art."

"There will be plenty of time for that," he said. "Now come."

He opened the cabinet on the side of the room. I saw a flash of leather: whips, rods, crops. Everything that he could use on me. Goosebumps ran down my arms. But what he took out was different.

I stared at it for a moment before realizing what it was.

"A… a collar?"

"I want you to put it on yourself," he said.

It wasn't a question. It was a command. But when he lifted the collar up for me to take, I saw in his eyes a flash of indecision. Before he could take it back, I reached out and took the collar.

The black leather was smooth, surprisingly smooth, and cool to the touch. Small diamond studs edged the outside of the leather strip.

"Matches my underwear," I said. "Would you hold my hair up while I put it on?"

Jake smiled, and a thought flashed through my mind: *I'd passed the last test.*

His warm hands smoothed back around my neck and gathered my hair up. I put the collar on and slipped the leather strap through its buckle.

"Not the tightest setting," Jake said, watching carefully as I put it on. "Leave yourself a bit of give. You'll want it."

I shook my hair out. Jake looked at me in wonder.

"You approve?" I asked teasingly.

When he spoke his voice was throaty.

"Very much so," he said.

He pulled a silk tie from his jacket.

"Is that…"

"A blindfold."

"Really?"

"I don't want you distracted. I want you to focus entirely on how it feels. There isn't a canvas on the ground tonight, and we're not performing for anyone."

He knotted the silk tie around my head, and everything was dark. His strong hands came around my waist and lifted me onto the bed.

"That's why you brought me here?" I was beginning to see the real person behind Jake Carville.

"I'm Jake out there. In here…"

"You're Kage," I finished. "I understand."

"You don't understand yet," he said. He sounded like he was smiling.

"This is the only place you let yourself go. This is how you relax," I said.

Blindfolded, I could only remember the way the art spattered over the concrete walls, the mirrored wall he'd broken. I remembered his face and how he'd looked at me when he first kissed me. Hungry. My heart beat faster.

"Most people lose control. You take it."

"That's true," he said, laughing softly. "But you forgot the most important thing of all."

"What's that?"

"In here, I allow myself to get creative."

The handcuffs slipped over my wrists. He'd padded them with silk, and I tugged gently. The chains clinked in the darkness. I breathed in and out, trying not to let panic overtake me. I was blind and bound; there was a collar around my neck, but this was Jake's house I was in. Jake's room. *He wouldn't harm me.*

The chains pulled my arms out and up, and I sat up on my knees. I swayed slightly, dizzy underneath the blindfold, but the handcuffs held me tightly enough so that I wouldn't fall.

I could feel his breathing on the back of my neck. I strained forward, away from him, but the ties around my wrists held fast. He had me. Oh, God, he had me now, and he could do whatever he wanted with me.

"Lacey, my darling." He breathed the words into my ear from behind me. I gasped as his hand touched my shoulder. His fingers were warmer than his breath on the back of my neck.

Kage.

"Are you afraid of the dark?"

I was terrified, but it wasn't because of the dark. I was terrified that this would be the last night he touched me. Tonight would be over soon, and then I would have to go back to my stupid jobs and my stupid life. More than that, I was scared to even think past this moment.

And I wondered what he would do to me now.

His fingers slid down my back. His other hand gripped my hip. The bed moved as he shifted his weight closer to me. I gritted my teeth. I was his, but only for one more night. What would he do to me now that he knew he could do anything?

Despite myself, I felt my body begin to respond as his hands curved down around my waist and paused there. Warmth spread between my thighs. I clenched them together tightly, trying to ignore the pulsing desire inside of me.

Take me. Take me.

No. This wasn't me. This couldn't be real. The Lacey who walked into this apartment would never have let someone put a collar around her neck. And yet here I was, with the pressure of the leather strap around my neck. With chains binding my arms out to the sides.

Who was I?

I jerked my head away at the sudden touch on my neck. Even in the darkness, I could tell that he was smiling behind me. The touch came again, and this time I was prepared.

260

But then his lips pressed against my neck. I tried to sit still, but he sucked at my skin and I couldn't help the moan that tore from my collared throat.

"Oh, Lacey," he murmured.

His hands came forward, sliding over my stomach and up to my breasts. Again he kissed my neck. Again I gasped. This time it was his tongue, the hot pressure sending me into near spasms as he cupped my breasts.

I moaned as he sucked my skin and everything sank into pure sensation—

—his muscled chest against my back, his skin hot against mine—

—his fingers pinching my nipples so hard it sends flames racing through my nerves, his thumb rolling over the hard swollen nubs—

—his lips taking me, his mouth possessing me, his tongue licking my skin—

—his breath whispering softness into my ear—

"I can't stop myself," he said.

Oh God. Oh, Jake. If there was anything in the world I wanted right now, it was his cock inside of me. My body ached to take him inside, thick and pulsing.

"Don't try," I rasped.

Don't. I didn't want him to stop. Not now. I wanted him to do everything to me. I didn't want him to hold back anymore. He wasn't Jake anymore, he was Kage, and I wanted everything that he had to offer.

Still, it was this delicious anticipation that built the pressure inside of me, that rolled over and through my nerves. His hands came down, gripping my thighs. His fingers scrabbled needily over my skin. Before I could say another word, he forced my thighs apart.

I wanted him so badly, but I wanted him to want me the same way.

My body recoiled, clenching together, but he was already kneeling between my legs behind me. His hard cock pressed against the small of my back. It was impossibly hot, burning hot against my cool skin. I moaned as he slid his cock down between my thighs to where I was already slick with moisture.

"Jesus. Oh Jesus. Lacey." His voice was a growl that sent shivers through my body. "You don't know what you do to me."

What I do to you? Lord, what have you done to me? Before I came into this place, I did not know what sex felt like. I didn't know what it felt like to be taken, possessed, by someone determined to have every inch of my body for his own.

My fingers grasped at the handcuffs, but they were already pulled taut. My body, too, felt like it was pulled taut, waiting for his touch to send me into uncontrollable vibrations.

I closed my eyes. It didn't matter; the blindfold was still on, but this felt like the last decision I could make. I made it silently, the words curling through my mind and stopping before they reached my tongue.

Take me. Take me into your darkness.

He paused at my entrance, and then his arms came around me from behind, holding me tight. He slid into me, slowly, deliberately slowly, and stopped before he'd pierced me even halfway.

"What do you feel, Lacey?" he asked. "Let it take you over. Whatever you feel, let yourself feel it completely. Don't hold back."

I bit my lip, aching to scream. He was inside of me, yes, but now that I could feel him, I wanted more. I wanted every part of him on me, inside me.

"I feel... you," I choked out. "You're so big. I want it. I want... I want you."

"No pain?"

I shook my head, biting my lip. It was anguish to wait, yes, but apart from that exquisite sensation, there was no pain. Only the best kind of pressure.

His hands cupped my breast, and then he thrust upward, impaling me. I cried out in ecstasy at the feeling of being completely filled, and then he twisted my nipple and I screamed.

"This is much better than having you gagged, don't you think?" Jake whispered. I couldn't answer. I was panting, squirming, my heart pounding in my ears.

He rocked back down, and I moaned as he thrust upward again. His muscled chest pressed against my back and the chains that were holding me creaked as he lifted my weight from the binding and let it down, over and over again.

He moved slowly, impossibly slowly. I hated him for it, and loved him for it, because every motion of his sent slow thrills through my nerve endings. I felt his cock as it worked deeper and deeper inside of me. His fingers as they rolled my nipples, twisting and pinching to send shocks of pleasure through my chest. His mouth on the back of my neck, nibbling just above the line of the collar.

The delicious friction of his motion built up a pressure that grew and grew, making me dizzy with anticipation. He was taking me from behind, and he hadn't yet touched me in the front. I didn't know what he was doing, but I trusted him, and the fear racing through my body made the sensations all the more intense.

Again and again he thrust up into me, until his cock was slick with my juices and I was moaning and twisting at the chains. I was on the verge of orgasm when my throat was suddenly choked. I gasped, feeling the thick leather collar pull my head back.

"Don't you dare come without telling me," he whispered. "You know that, Lacey."

"Please—" I gasped. The collar was tight around my neck. He'd hooked his fingers into the back. That's why he'd had me leave space.

"I'm going to ride you now," he said. "You see how this collar pulls you?"

I nodded, gulping.

"I'm going to take you the way I want you," he growled. My heart skipped as he spoke. "And when I shoot into you, then you can come. Understood?"

"Understood," I whispered.

He yanked my collar back and I felt myself pulled off balance. The chains were the only things holding me up. He'd leaned back, and then—

"AH!"

He spanked me, and I jerked, more in surprise than in pain. His cock thrust farther into me, and then he leaned back and spanked me again.

"God, I love the way you clench around me when I spank you," he said. He spanked me again, and I moaned. I was so wet, so hot, and I needed him badly.

"So tight. So sweet."

He thrust up and then spanked me again, rocking back. Over and over, he repeated the motions, until the red pain of the spanks turned to bright sparks of pleasure. My hips bucked back to meet his thrusts and blows in alternating rhythm.

Oh, God, I couldn't last like this forever.

I was biting my lip to keep myself from climax. Every single one of his touches made the pressure build and build, and I began to moan with each thrust. He wasn't spanking me anymore; his rhythm had grown so fast that he had to hold my body tight to keep it from rocking too far away.

Faster and faster he moved, slamming his body into mine. His hands came around my wrists, and his legs forced my legs apart. He thrust up so hard that it took my weight off of the bed, and when I landed back he was there to meet me. His skin was slick with moisture against mine as he thrust faster, faster.

"God, please—"

"Oh, Lacey," he moaned, and I could feel his cock stiffen inside of me. He jerked once, upward, groaning—

"Ahhhh!"

It didn't take any time at all for me to let go. The pressure building inside of me exploded into a burst of sensation, and I screamed as I clenched and unclenched around his pulsing shaft. I could feel his hot seed spilling out as I fell over the edge into my own orgasm.

It was dark, but I could see bursts of color in the darkness as my body uncoiled into ecstasy. My fingers gripped the handcuffs and the collar around my throat pulled tightly. Every part of my body unraveled in pleasure, the orgasm spinning through me in waves of feeling. I was dizzy with pleasure.

My heart was pounding. All I could hear was his breaths and mine, but I felt my heart beat with a shudder of motion that pulsed through my whole body.

Soft kisses on the back of my shoulders brought me back to the world. Jake withdrew from me, and I felt his seed spill down the inside of my thigh. I licked my lips. They had gone dry with my rasping breaths.

Jake moved around to my front, his weight moving on the mattress. He uncuffed me, catching my body before I could fall onto the bed. He pushed the blindfold up over my eyes, and I blinked hard into the dazzling green irises.

"Lacey," he murmured. His eyes were only the slightest bit worried, but that was too much for me.

I leaned forward to kiss him, and he pulled me fully into his arms, taking my kiss and returning it tenfold. I couldn't breathe as his lips sought out mine, seizing them in a kiss so hard that it bruised. He pulled himself away with a sigh before planting a few more tender kisses alongside the line of my chin.

I let him take the collar off of me. My hands were shaking still, and my fingers weren't steady enough to unclasp the buckle. When he'd taken it off, I finally felt naked.

He held his hand out and I took it, letting him lead me to the door in a silent reflection of the pleasure he'd given me. He'd broken me into a thousand pieces and let me put myself back together with my own desires. He'd given me more than anyone else.

A pang of sorrow stabbed through me. I took one last longing look back at the room. The broken mirror reflecting Jake's art. His true self. I bit my lip and forced myself to ask him the question.

"You said that there will be plenty of time for me to see this art."

"That's right."

"Then... then you're not going to kick me out after this week is up?"

He took my face in his hands and kissed me. And in that kiss, I began to cry. Because I knew that he wasn't keeping me here as a playtoy to use for sex. There was sex, and it was fun, but there was more than that.

"Lacey," he said. "Look at me. Look at me."

I blinked back the tears and stared up into his face. My vision swam with blurry tears. But I could see his eyes, always his green eyes, gazing kindly back at me.

"Lacey, I love you. And I want you to stay here with me."

"You're sure?" I wiped away a tear. Oh, to be here with him! All of my worries dissolved into happiness.

"I've never been more certain of anything else in my life. Lacey, this is sudden. I know it's sudden. It's sudden for me, too. But there isn't anything I want to hold back from you. You've seen all sides of me, and you haven't batted an eyelash."

"Technically, I batted a few eyelashes," I said, laughing through my tears. "But you had me blindfolded so you couldn't see."

"Then you do want to stay?"

"With you?" I looked up at Jake's now-serious face.

"Of course," I said, my heart swelling with emotion. "I love you, too."

***

We walked out of the room side by side. I was giddy with pleasure, and I couldn't help the bounce in my step. Jake squeezed my fingers with his.

"If you want to stay, you can. The only thing we'll have to work out…"

"Yes?"

"Which one of us gets to use the art studio?" he asked, cocking his head.

"I'll get the mornings," I said.

"Oh? The morning light? All of it? You really think you're going to keep mornings?"

"You'll have to tie me up and drag me out of there kicking and screaming," I said.

"I accept your terms," he said, grinning.

"It's your fault, really," I teased. "You make me want to paint nonstop."

"Painting, huh? Is that what the kids call it nowadays?"

Laughing, hand in hand, we walked down the hallway to whatever the future held for us.

***

Thank you for reading His Gift!

If you enjoyed the story would you please consider leaving a review on your favorite retailer?
Just a few words and some stars really does help!

Be sure to find out about new releases, deals and giveaways, by hopping on my mailing list!
http://bit.ly/AubreyDarkNewsletter

Find out what happens next in the sequel!
HIS RANSOM

Some secrets are darker than others...

I knew that there was more to billionaire Jake Carville than what he showed the world. But I didn't know that Jake's past was so dark... and so dangerous.

Lacey Miller is just a curvy girl, a tomboy, a street artist. When she steps into Jake Carville's life, his obsession with her will lead her into a world like she's never seen. A world of wealth and power. A world of unquenchable passion and unspeakable cruelty.

Jake Carville, billionaire playboy, has never found a woman he can open up to. Not until Lacey. She's the only woman he cares about. His gift. His love.

… and that's why she's the perfect hostage.

Out now on Createspace and Amazon!

Get a sneak peek with this sample of HIS RANSOM:

Chapter One

"Your body is a work of art, Lacey."

Jake hugged me around the middle as he craned over to kiss my neck. I squinted at the large unfinished painting in front of me, trying not to succumb to his distractions. I dabbed the palette knife into black paint, tilting my head to see the painting better, and also to let his mouth taste the full side of my throat.

No. Try as I might, I couldn't ignore him. Flames of heat licked through my nerves at the touch of his lips.

I couldn't ignore the way his hands slid up the front of my shirt. I couldn't ignore his palms pressing hot and wanting against my chest. I sighed as he cupped my breasts, squeezing them lightly. His hands were so warm against my skin. And his lips...

"I need to finish this," I said, trying really hard to frown.

"Why?"

"The gallery said they wanted something new to put out front."

And I wanted something new to give them.

Apart from the few sales Jake had made at the opening show, there had been no interest from art collectors who looked through the gallery. It was stupid of me to be so disappointed, but I hadn't made a single sale on my own in the past month. I felt like a failure.

"You can finish the painting," Jake said. His fingers flew down to my pants, unzipping my jeans and tugging at the waistline. "You won't even notice I'm here."

"I really doubt that," I said. I turned back to the painting, tugging my jeans up with my free hand and dabbing at the canvas with the palette knife. Should there be more red on the background?

I didn't know. This, more than anything else, was what made me mad. I was getting all mixed up, trying to figure out what the gallery owners would be able to sell.

Before, my paintings had been all about what I wanted to do. I put my pieces up on subway cars and alleyways. I didn't care about what anyone thought. I painted flowers because I wanted to paint flowers.

All that had changed. Since Jake rented out the art gallery for me, I felt more and more pressure to do things a certain way. Not my way.

I frowned as Jake's hands slid my jeans down over my hips. All this attention was taking my focus away from where it should have been—on the painting.

"Seriously, Jake," I said.

"Jake's not here," Jake whispered. His hand slid down over the front of my panties, and despite myself, I gasped in pleasure. The touch of his fingers sent my body into a state of high alert. Every nerve trembled.

"Then whose hands are these?" I asked, my breath coming faster as he slid his hands over me. The slightest brush of his fingers against my front was enough to send my heart racing.

"Nobody's. There's nobody here. You just keep painting." He spoke the words softly as he nudged the hem of my panties down with one thumb.

I reached out, gritting my teeth and swiping a palette knife full of black across the middle. I had no idea what I was doing, and right now I didn't care. Jake was sending my body into an unbearable state of desire. I didn't care about the painting anymore. I just wanted to be done.

A hiss of air through Jake's teeth had me looking back over my shoulder. He was staring at the line my palette knife had taken.

"What?" I said, putting my hand on my hip.

"Nothing."

"It's not nothing. Do you hate it?" I tried to turn around, but my jeans were bunched down around my knees and I lurched backward, off balance. Jake caught me. His strong arms lifted me up to face him.

"I don't hate it," he said. He pushed me back.

I eyed the painting over my shoulder. From this angle it became even more apparent that the darn thing sucked.

"It's horrible."

"It's not horrible," Jake said. He paused, tilting his head. "But that line is a bit out of place, don't you think?"

"Oh." It was a grunt of defeat.

"Not that out of place," Jake said, attempting to backpedal. "It's fine, really."

"I'm a bit out of place," I grumbled. Jake giving me fake praise was worse than his criticism.

"What?"

"Nothing!" I cried.

"Are you really upset with me now?" Jake asked incredulously.

"Look, you can't come in here and start kissing me and messing up my concentration and... and then critiquing my painting while I'm painting the dang thing!"

"You're right," Jake said, raising his hands in mock surrender.

"I am."

"Yes. And you should stop painting for now."

"I know. Wait, what?"

But Jake had already plucked the palette knife from my hand. He tossed it down and shoved me back against the canvas. I squealed, feeling the paint squelch through the fabric of my shirt.

"Ahh—" My cry was cut off by the crash of his lips onto mine. I moaned and he deepened the kiss, his hands moving down over my body quickly. Every touch sent a new burst of fire through my nervous system. I'd thought that after a month of sleeping with this man, my desire would have started to die down. Instead, I only wanted him more.

I could feel his need in the way he tore his kisses from my lips, his mouth burning on mine. I needed him, too. As he tore off his shirt, I stepped quickly out of my pants. He unbuckled his belt.

"God," I said, gasping for breath. "I can't—please—"

I turned, my hair sticking to the wet canvas. It was smudged beyond repair. Jake shoved my shoulder back, pinning me with his broad hand to the painting that was now completely wrecked.

"Oh, ohh—"

His lips pressed onto my neck again. His teeth nibbled the hard line of my collarbone all the way down to the hollow in the middle of my shoulders. I gave up trying to save the painting. It was lost. My hands threaded through his hair, pulling him close. I could feel his hardness through his pants. God, I was so wet.

How could a man do this? He turned me on and teased me to the edge of insanity with his lips. As he kissed me, he pushed and pulled, leading me past desire and into a crazed passion. My lips trembled against his.

Then his hand was shoving his pants down, exposing his hard cock. I barely had time to take a breath before he was on me, forcing between my thighs. I cried out as he thrust upward, smearing paint vertically with my whole body as the brush. His cock pushed through my entrance roughly.

"Ahhh!" I cried, feeling his thickness inside me. He was hard as steel, and his thrusts lifted me up. I stood on tiptoe, rocking back down with his already-quickening rhythm. I placed my hands against his broad shoulders, trying to balance.

"Jesus, Lacey, you're so damn tight," Jake said. His hand slid over my ass, gripping the curves there. He gave a quick spank and I squealed.

"I love it when you do that," I gasped.

Jake's eyes twinkled green from under his tousled hair. I could see the beginning darkness of sweat at his hairline as he began to move inside me.

"I love it more," he said. He spanked me again, and I clenched. The sharp thrill of pain gave way to an even more intense pleasure as he kneaded my ass with his strong fingers.

Another spank.

"You tighten up every time I do that," he said, smiling. His eyes were wide pools of pleasure as he thrust upward again, this time slowly, easing his length into me. I moaned. He spanked me again.

"Maybe it's just you getting bigger," I said breathlessly. He grinned.

"God, you're perfect," he said. He pressed a kiss onto the top of my head as he thrust into me, rolling his hips. I gasped as his muscles brushed the top of my swollen flesh, sending me almost over the edge. I drew a ragged breath as he rocked back.

Perfect. I had never heard myself described that way before. My body was all curves and swells, nothing you would find in a magazine model. And yet when Jake looked at me, touched me, I felt that he was telling the truth—that I was perfect for him.

"Lacey," he moaned. He placed one hand against the canvas and rolled into me again. I heard the hitching of his breath that told me he was close to orgasm. My leg came up around his thigh and he gripped it with his free hand. He pushed in even deeper. I clenched, feeling the growing ache of pressure inside of me. We would both be there soon.

"Take me," I whispered. I took his bottom lip between mine and sucked hard. He groaned.

He rocked into me, bracing himself against the canvas. His body slid over mine, his hands holding me up even as my legs went liquid. The pressure in me was too high, too high. He drew back from a kiss and put his forehead to mine, staring me in the eyes.

"Now," he said, his voice a growl. "Come for me."

I inhaled a gasp at his words, and as he plunged deep into me I screamed. I was over the edge, flinging myself headlong into ecstasy. Explosions of pleasure burst through my nerves as he thrust again and again. I held onto his arms for dear life as the climax shuddered through me.

Jake pulled my leg around him and thrust quickly once, then twice. I heard him take a breath and then felt his hot seed as he stilled, his orgasm right on the heels of mine. He was hard, steel-hard, jerking inside of me as his whole body rippled with pleasure.

"Oh, Lacey—" he moaned. He reached around, cupping my head and tilting it up for another kiss.

I kissed him back helplessly, my body too weak to do anything but collapse willingly into his arms. We both slid down the canvas to the ground in a tangle of paint-splattered arms and legs, him kissing me all the while.

My heart returned to normal after a couple of minutes, and I felt a chill in the air as he lifted his arm from across my body.

He kissed me softly and then arched his head back, looking at the painting. I looked with him. The black line had been almost completely smudged over. Heck, most of the painting had been completely smudged over.

There were two handprints—one Jake's, where he had braced himself. One mine, where I had clawed down during my orgasm. And my hair had dragged down a huge smear of red from the top.

"It's ruined, isn't it?" I asked.

"I don't know," Jake said, tilting his head again, this time the other way. "I think I like it with the smears like that."

"Really?"

"Really," he said, looking down at me with a grin. "And I think we should definitely have a celebration orgasm for you."

"A celebration what?"

His hands began to move, stirring the heat inside me, and I wriggled under his grasp. I could feel myself getting ready for more.

"To celebrate another finished painting."

His mouth came down on me again, and I let myself fall into his embrace.

Grab His Ransom now on Createspace or Amazon - FREE in Kindle Unlimited